In the Line of Duty . . .

Bullets whistled past his head as he dived behind a table, upsetting it as he landed. He rolled, stuck his gun around the overturned table, and triggered twice.

The members of Horne's gang were fleeing by now, including the men who'd been throwing back drinks at the bar. One of them staggered and grabbed at his left thigh as Longarm's slug drilled through it.

The others reached a rear door and ducked through it. Bert Collins started after them, calling to Longarm, "I'll go after 'em this way! Circle around back, Long!"

Longarm might have done that if he hadn't seen a flicker of movement in the shadows at the far end of the room. A staircase there led up to a narrow balcony, and a man had just stepped out onto that balcony.

The newcomer had a revolver in each hand, and the six-guns roared thunderously, drowning out the warning that Longarm tried to call to his fellow deputy marshal.

Collins stumbled as the slugs punched into him. The man on the balcony ripped off half a dozen shots, and every one of them hit Collins. Momentum carried him for a few steps before he lost his balance and pitched forward on his face.

→·◆ **TABOR EVANS** ◆·←

LONGARM

AND THE
PANAMINT PANIC

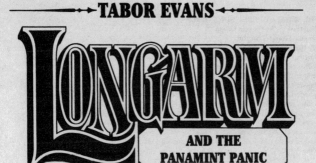

J
JOVE BOOKS, NEW YORK

THE BERKLEY PUBLISHING GROUP
Published by the Penguin Group
Penguin Group (USA) Inc.
375 Hudson Street, New York, New York 10014, USA

Penguin Group (Canada), 90 Eglinton Avenue East, Suite 700, Toronto, Ontario M4P 2Y3, Canada
(a division of Pearson Penguin Canada Inc.)
Penguin Books Ltd., 80 Strand, London WC2R 0RL, England
Penguin Group Ireland, 25 St. Stephen's Green, Dublin 2, Ireland (a division of Penguin Books Ltd.)
Penguin Group (Australia), 250 Camberwell Road, Camberwell, Victoria 3124, Australia
(a division of Pearson Australia Group Pty. Ltd.)
Penguin Books India Pvt. Ltd., 11 Community Centre, Panchsheel Park, New Delhi—110 017, India
Penguin Group (NZ), 67 Apollo Drive, Rosedale, North Shore 0632, New Zealand
(a division of Pearson New Zealand Ltd.)
Penguin Books (South Africa) (Pty.) Ltd., 24 Sturdee Avenue, Rosebank, Johannesburg 2196,
South Africa

Penguin Books Ltd., Registered Offices: 80 Strand, London WC2R 0RL, England

This is a work of fiction. Names, characters, places, and incidents either are the product of the author's imagination or are used fictitiously, and any resemblance to actual persons, living or dead, business establishments, events, or locales is entirely coincidental.

LONGARM AND THE PANAMINT PANIC

A Jove Book / published by arrangement with the author

PRINTING HISTORY
Jove edition / February 2011

Copyright © 2011 by Penguin Group (USA) Inc.
Cover illustration by Milo Sinovcic.

ISBN: 978-0-515-14898-5

JOVE®
Jove Books are published by The Berkley Publishing Group,
a division of Penguin Group (USA) Inc.,
375 Hudson Street, New York, New York 10014.
JOVE® is a registered trademark of Penguin Group (USA) Inc.
The "J" design is a trademark of Penguin Group (USA) Inc.

PRINTED IN THE UNITED STATES OF AMERICA

10 9 8 7 6 5 4 3 2 1

Chapter 1

Longarm swung down from the train onto the platform of the El Paso depot and turned to help a woman disembark after him.

Her name was Juliet McAdams. Longarm had met her on the trip down from Denver, and her blond beauty and sweet smile had made the time pass much more pleasantly.

Not to mention the heat of her mouth when her lips were wrapped around his cock.

She smiled now and squeezed his hand. "I wish we'd had the chance to get to know each other better, Custis."

"So do I," he told her honestly. "Maybe we'll run into each other again one of these days."

"Not unless you come into my uncle's hardware store." Juliet was moving to El Paso from Pueblo and had a job waiting for her in her uncle's business.

"Well, that could happen," Longarm said. "A man never knows when he might need a screw."

She laughed delightedly. "You're awful, Custis."

"Yeah, but I have my endearin' qualities," he replied with a grin.

She rubbed her hand up and down his arm, squeezing it through the sleeve of the brown tweed suit. "Indeed you do," she said fervently. "Indeed you do."

They might have lingered over their good-byes even longer, but Longarm caught sight of a familiar face coming toward him along the platform.

Bert Collins was a deputy United States marshal, too. Longarm's boss, Chief Marshal Billy Vail, had told him that Collins would meet him here in El Paso.

He leaned forward, pressed his lips to Juliet's as he held her shoulders, then said, "So long, darlin'. It's been a pleasure."

He thought he saw a flash of regret in her blue eyes. "A real pleasure," she murmured.

Longarm didn't expect the next few days to be nearly as enjoyable as the trip down from Denver, since he and Bert Collins were faced with the task of tracking down and capturing or killing a bunch of ruthless owlhoots.

He turned to nod a greeting to his fellow deputy. Collins was a stocky, medium-sized man with a black mustache that drooped over his wide mouth. He wore an old black Stetson with a round crown, a red shirt with a black leather vest over it, and jeans tucked into stovepipe boots. He looked more a cowboy than a federal lawman.

Longarm often dressed like a cowboy, too, when he was on a job, but tonight he was rigged out in a fancier getup, the sort of suit that President Hayes's wife Lucy thought all federal employees should wear so they would look like respectable representatives of the government.

Lemonade Lucy generally got what she wanted, so the directive had gone out. Longarm wore a brown tweed suit with a matching vest, black boots, and a flat-crowned, snuff brown hat. A gold chain looped across the front of his vest from one pocket to the other. At one end of the chain was a big gold turnip watch that kept perfect time.

At the other end, its butt welded to the chain, was a two-shot derringer that had saved Longarm's bacon more than once when some hombre who wanted him dead believed him to be unarmed.

He also wore a Colt .44 double-action revolver in a cross-draw rig on his left hip. He was fast and slick on the draw with it, although he had never wasted even a moment's thought on how his speed stacked up against that of the famous gunfighters who had risen to prominence in the West over the past decade.

He was fast enough to have stayed alive this long, and that was all that mattered.

Longarm howdied and shook with Collins. "Good to see you again, Bert," he said. "You ready to get on the trail of Gideon Horne and the rest of that bunch of no-goods?"

Collins gave him a tight-lipped smile. "Don't have to get on Horne's trail," he said. "I know where he is."

Longarm stiffened slightly in surprise. "You know where he is?" he repeated.

Collins nodded. "Yeah. Right here in El Paso, at a place called Mama Lupe's down on Stanton Street."

Longarm recalled hearing about Mama Lupe's from previous visits to the border town, although he had never been there. It was supposed to be one of the best whorehouses in either El Paso or Juarez, across the river.

Just the sort of place where a train robber with ill-gotten loot burning a hole in his pocket might choose to spend some time.

If he was a damn fool, that is.

"Are you tellin' me that Horne and his wild bunch didn't light a shuck for Mexico as soon as they held up that train in Sierra Blanca?"

"That's right," replied Collins. "Shocked the dog-water out of me, too. That's where we all figured they'd head straightaway."

Longarm nodded. Gideon Horne and the gang of owl-hoots he led had taken over the depot at Sierra Blanca, in West Texas, a couple of nights earlier and boarded a westbound train when it stopped there.

The details had been in the report Billy Vail had showed Longarm when assigning him to the case. The train was carrying a good-sized money shipment, all of which had been looted by Horne and his gang. They had also stolen the mail pouches, which made the robbery a federal matter.

If the idiots had headed for the Rio Grande right then and there, they would have been south of the border long before any authorities could arrive on the scene and might have spent the rest of their lives there, enjoying the hot sun and the warm señoritas.

The fact that they had ridden to El Paso instead was just further proof that outlaws usually weren't the bright-est folks in the world.

"How'd you find out they were here?" Longarm asked Collins.

"I know a fella who works as a bartender at Mama Lupe's," the other deputy marshal replied. "He heard the news about what happened at Sierra Blanca, overheard the varmints talking enough to realize who they were, and got word to me."

Longarm nodded slowly. Collins had worked a lot of cases in West Texas and along the border, so he had a number of contacts in the area.

That had paid off in a big way in this instance. Long-arm had anticipated trailing the thieves to the Rio Grande and then having to decide whether he wanted to notify the Mexican rurales or bend the rules, cross the river, and go after Horne's bunch himself.

Now it appeared he wouldn't have to face that tough decision. If he and Collins could arrest the outlaws at Mama Lupe's, they wouldn't have to leave American soil.

"The report I read said that there were eleven men at the depot in Sierra Blanca. Those aren't very good odds. You reckon we can get some help from the local star packers?"

Collins nodded. "The sheriff's already promised me half a dozen deputies."

"And I'll bet a hat he wants the credit, too."

"You know Billy doesn't care about anything except catching the varmints and recovering the money," Collins said with a shrug. "Anyway, any prisoners we take will be locked up in the sheriff's jail, so that'll get him some notoriety no matter what we do."

"Yeah, it don't really matter," Longarm agreed. Sheriff was an elected position, so that meant the stink of politics inevitably crept in, whoever was doing the job. Longarm had learned to hold his nose and ignore it as best he could.

The train would be pulling out soon. "Let me get my saddle, rifle, and war-bag," Longarm went on. "Don't look like I'll need 'em this go-round, but you never know."

He reclaimed his gear from the baggage car and stowed it behind the window with the ticket clerk after identifying himself as a federal lawman.

Then he and Collins left the train station and walked toward the Rio Grande, several blocks away.

"This bartender at Mama Lupe's, you trust him enough to know he's not settin' up some sort of trap?" asked Longarm.

"He's never steered me wrong before," Collins said. "He's got no reason to now. There's already a reward for Horne's capture and the recovery of the loot, you know. Money can make even a dishonest man tell the truth."

Longarm knew that was right.

Half a dozen men stepped out from the shadows in front of a photographic studio that was closed for the night. "Collins," one of them said. "Is this the man you were expecting?"

"Yeah," Collins said. He jerked a thumb at Longarm. "Deputy Marshal Custis Long."

"Better known as Longarm," the man said. He held out his hand. "I'm Fred Benton, deputy sheriff here. These other fellas work for the sheriff, too. Harper, Rollinson, Guzman, Stengard, and Lopez."

Longarm nodded to the men and said, "Pleased to meet you, gents. You know what we're fixin' to get into?"

"A shoot-out, more than likely," one of the men replied. "Horne's bunch outnumbers us, and I don't expect they'll want to come along peaceable-like."

"Probably not," Longarm agreed. "But the place they're holed up at is a whorehouse, after all. Chances are at least some of them will be upstairs beddin' the girls who work there. If we take 'em by surprise, maybe we can nab some of the bunch before the others even know what's goin' on."

"Sounds like a good plan to me," Collins said with a nod. "Marshal Long and I aren't known there as lawmen, so we'll go in first. That way we'll already be in position when the rest of you make your move."

Benton returned the nod. "All right. We'll give you, what, ten minutes?"

"That ought to be long enough," Collins said.

The local lawmen drew back into the shadows as

Longarm and Collins walked on down the street toward Mama Lupe's.

It was a two-story adobe structure, Longarm saw when they got there, rather sedate-looking actually, with nothing to indicate it was a brothel except for a small red light burning discreetly in a second-floor window. A place like this relied on word of mouth to bring in the customers.

The architecture was Spanish-influenced. An adobe wall with a wooden gate in it encircled the property. The two lawmen walked up to the gate. Collins rapped a brass knocker on the panel.

A moment later, a latch rattled and the gate swung back. An extremely large Mexican man stood there. He didn't seem to be armed, but his bulging muscles were enough to make anybody think twice about starting trouble with him.

The man smiled and said in flawless, unaccented English, "Good evening, gentlemen. You seek pleasant companionship for the evening?"

"That's right," Collins said. "We've heard that this place has, uh, the most pleasant companionship in El Paso."

"*Es verdad.* Come in."

The guard stepped back to let them walk through the gate. Longarm hoped that the hombre wouldn't take a hand when it came time to deal with Gideon Horne and the rest of the outlaws. He and his fellow lawmen would have a big enough challenge just facing off against the gang.

"Right this way, señors," the guard said, ushering them along a passage with an arched roof that led to an open courtyard with fruit trees, flower beds, and a round fountain in the center.

Half a dozen attractive young women who wore only

short, sheer gowns lounged on the wide marble wall around the fountain. They all smiled seductively at the two lawmen.

Longarm had to admit that when it came to elegance and sensuality, Mama Lupe, whoever she was, seemed to know what she was doing. The warm night air was full of jasmine and romance, or rather, lust disguised as romance, and the combination would be overpowering to most men who visited here.

Longarm was affected pretty strongly himself. He found himself wishing he could just while away a few hours here, instead of having to instigate a possibly deadly showdown with a bunch of dirty owlhoots.

"You can take your pick of the señoritas, gentlemen," the guard said.

"You got a place where a man can get a drink first?" asked Longarm. He put a grin on his face. "I reckon I could do with a little fortifyin'. Wouldn't want to run out of strength too soon."

"Of course," the man said. "Right this way."

None of Horne's men were in the courtyard, no customers at all, in fact. Longarm wanted to get as many of the outlaws located as he could before Benton and the sheriff's other deputies came in here and things started to pop.

The guard led them through another passage into a smoky barroom, where the drink juggler behind the hardwood glanced at them but kept his face carefully expressionless. That would be the hombre who had tipped off Collins, thought Longarm.

Several men stood at a bar that ran along the right side of the room. Four more sat at a table and played poker.

Collins glanced over at Longarm and gave him a tiny nod, signifying that all of these were Horne's men.

Gideon Horne himself was the only one Longarm might have recognized, because he had read a good description of the man in the paperwork on the case. Horne was about thirty, a handsome man with a distinctive white streak in his dark hair.

Longarm didn't see the boss outlaw anywhere in the room and assumed that Horne was upstairs sporting with one of Mama Lupe's girls.

That was as far as Longarm's thoughts got before he realized that he did recognize one of the men at the poker table after all. The man's name was Frank Denkinger, and Longarm had arrested him a few years earlier for stagecoach robbery.

Denkinger must have either busted out of prison or gotten a lighter sentence than Longarm would have handed out if it was up to him, because here he was in El Paso, having thrown in with Gideon Horne.

That wasn't the worst of it. Denkinger recognized him, too.

The outlaw's eyes widened for a second, then he surged up out of his chair, clawing at the gun on his hip as he yelled, "That's a fuckin' lawman who just walked in!"

Chapter 2

This wasn't the first time Longarm had run into a bad break like this. He'd had such a long, busy career as a badge toter that the frontier was littered with men he'd arrested and vengeful relatives of varmints he'd had to kill.

Now, faced with this dilemma again, he did the only thing he could.

He pulled iron and put a .44 slug right through the son of a bitch's brain pan.

The other three men at the table lurched upright and slapped leather, too. Longarm lunged to his left and fired again while he was on the move, but this shot missed.

Bert Collins drew his gun and went the other way, blasting a couple of shots at the outlaws. Longarm saw one of them double over and collapse.

Bullets whistled past his head as he dived behind a table, upsetting it as he landed. He rolled, stuck his gun around the overturned table, and triggered twice.

The members of Horne's gang were fleeing by now, including the men who'd been throwing back drinks at the bar. One of them staggered and grabbed at his left thigh as Longarm's slug drilled through it.

The others reached a rear door and ducked through it. Bert Collins started after them, calling to Longarm, "I'll go after 'em this way! Circle around back, Long!"

Longarm might have done that if he hadn't seen a flicker of movement in the shadows at the far end of the room. A staircase there led up to a narrow balcony, and a man had just stepped out onto that balcony.

The newcomer had a revolver in each hand, and the six-guns roared thunderously, drowning out the warning that Longarm tried to call to his fellow deputy marshal.

Collins stumbled as the slugs punched into him. The man on the balcony ripped off half a dozen shots, and every one of them hit Collins. Momentum carried him for a few steps before he lost his balance and pitched forward on his face.

Longarm angled his .44 up and fired again, the bullet coming close enough that the gunman on the balcony was forced to jump back into the dark hallway from which he had emerged when the shooting started.

Unfortunately, that shot emptied the cylinder of Longarm's Colt, so he had to roll behind the table again to dump the brass and thumb fresh cartridges from his shell belt into the gun.

Elsewhere in the house, women screamed and men shouted startled curses and questions. Longarm heard the pound of running feet. He ducked his head lower as shots blasted from the stairs and bullets chewed splinters from the overturned table behind which he crouched.

Even though the light was poor, Longarm had caught a glimpse of the white streak in the hair of the man who had shot Bert Collins. The man was Gideon Horne himself, and now the boss outlaw was making a break for it. Longarm heard his hurried footsteps coming down the stairs.

Longarm holstered his gun and grabbed the legs of the table he was using for cover. Calling on all the strength in his rangy, danger-hardened body, he powered to his feet and flung the table at the staircase.

The move seemed to take Horne completely by surprise as he reached the bottom of the stairs. He jerked up his guns and triggered both of them as the table sailed at him, but of course the slugs didn't stop it.

The table crashed into him and knocked him back on the steps.

Longarm sprang after it, eager to close with the outlaw. By now, Fred Benton and the other deputies outside should have heard the shooting and come a-runnin'. Longarm would have to rely on them to round up the rest of the gang.

He wanted Gideon Horne for himself, the murdering bastard.

He would have gotten Horne, who was stunned by the impact of the table hitting him, if not for the man Longarm had wounded in the leg a few moments earlier. The man reached up and grabbed Longarm's leg as he ran past.

Taken by surprise, Longarm crashed to the floor. His gun slipped out of his fingers and skidded away across the sawdust-littered planks.

The wounded man clutched at him and tried to clamber up and stab the lawman with a knife he'd pulled from a sheath at his belt. Longarm twisted and shot his left arm out.

His hand closed around the man's wrist before the knife could fall. With his right, he threw a short, hard right that landed cleanly on the outlaw's jaw and slewed his head to the side. The man's eyes rolled up in their sockets, and he dropped the knife.

That left Horne to deal with, and as Longarm craned

his neck and twisted his head around to look up the stairs, he saw that the boss outlaw had recovered and was drawing a bead on him. Longarm knew he had only a split-second to live.

In that split-second, Benton and some of the other deputies burst into the room with their guns blazing. Horne never pulled the trigger. He had to throw himself backward to avoid the hail of lead that suddenly stormed around him.

Catching himself on one hand to keep his balance, he dashed back up the stairs to the second floor. Bullets struck all around him, chipping plaster from the wall and throwing white dust in the air, but Horne never slowed.

He was the luckiest son of a bitch who'd ever lived, thought Longarm, to escape that fusillade.

Horne disappeared down the upstairs hallway. "Get after him!" Benton yelled, and several of the deputies rushed for the stairs.

Benton reached Longarm's side as the federal lawman got to his feet. "Wasn't that Horne?"

Longarm nodded grimly. "It sure was. Bastard ventilated Collins."

A bitter curse came from Benton. "I'll check on him, if you want to get after Horne."

"Much obliged," Longarm said. He didn't think there was anything anybody could do for Collins, not the way he'd been shot through the body half a dozen times, but somebody needed to be sure.

Meanwhile, Longarm scooped up his gun from the floor, then turned and ran back out through the front of the whorehouse.

He didn't see the big bouncer or the bartender anywhere on his way out. Those hombres had had sense enough to lie low while hell was on the prowl and gun thunder filled the air.

All the nearly naked girls in the courtyard had scattered, too, a wise move on their part.

When Longarm reached the street, he turned and ran along the adobe wall. There had to be some sort of stable in the back where the outlaws had kept their mounts.

Longarm knew Gideon Horne would try to get to his horse and flee across the border, which was what he should have done a couple of nights earlier. Reaching the stable first was Longarm's best chance of stopping him.

Longarm made it to the rear corner of the building in time to see Horne burst out of a ramshackle barn on horseback. A couple of deputies emerged from the back door of the house at that moment and opened fire.

Horne hauled hard on the reins and whirled his mount away from the flying lead.

That sent him toward Longarm, who brought his Colt up and fired. Horne ducked just as Longarm squeezed the trigger, though. Longarm had to leap aside to avoid being trampled before he could fire a second shot.

Lying on the filthy floor of the back alley, Longarm rolled over and aimed as best he could in the bad light. He triggered the .44 again and again.

Horne veered hard to the right and cut up another alley. Longarm heard more shots and figured Benton's men had gotten in Horne's way. He scrambled to his feet and gave chase.

As he came back out onto Stanton Street, he saw Horne heading north. The deputies had cut him off from the Rio Grande.

Benton ran along the street, shouting, "Get to the river! Block the bridges! Don't let Horne get across!"

That sounded like a good idea to Longarm.

He didn't know where the rest of the gang had gone. Some or all of them had probably succeeded in reaching

Mexico. Longarm didn't like that. Letting any outlaw escape justice was a bitter pill for him to swallow.

But he would trade all of them for that lawman-murdering Gideon Horne, he thought as he went up to Benton.

"How's Collins?" he asked, figuring that he already knew the answer.

"Sorry, Marshal," the local lawman said. "He never had a chance. He was shot to pieces. Did Horne do it?"

Longarm nodded. "Yeah. Son of a bitch came out on that balcony above the barroom with a smokepole in each hand and cut loose his wolf."

"Well, he won't get away," Benton promised. "There are only a couple of bridges across the river, and we'll cover 'em both."

"What if he tries to swim across?"

"Then he'll likely drown. The Rio's up and flowing strong right now because of the spring thaw in the Rockies. A man would have to be a fool to try to swim it."

"Or desperate enough," Longarm muttered.

"Well, if he does try, we'll find his body washed up downstream in a day or so."

"What about the others?"

Benton shook his head. "They got away before we could stop them. They're over in Mexico by now."

Longarm thought of something. "Except for the pair we killed and the one I plugged in the leg."

"Yeah, that's right. There's a live one still inside. I've got Lupe sitting on him."

"The madam?"

Benton laughed humorlessly. "There isn't any madam. Guadalupe Garza runs this place. Reckon you probably met him when you went in."

"That great big hombre? That's Mama Lupe?"

"Yeah. He's not real fond of gals, if you get my drift, Long. I guess that makes him the perfect fella to run a whorehouse. He's never tempted to sample the goods."

Longarm blew out his breath and shook his head. It took all kinds in this world. He said, "I want to go talk to him."

"Lupe?"

"No, the fella I plugged in the leg."

They went inside and found Guadalupe Garza sitting in a chair in the barroom with a big foot planted firmly on the back of the injured man, who lay facedown. The bodies of the two outlaws Longarm and Collins had killed lay nearby.

The wounded outlaw had regained consciousness after Longarm knocked him out, and he was complaining bitterly.

"—gonna bleed to death, I tell you," he was saying. "I need a doctor!"

"Yeah, you need to be patched up so you'll be in good health when you hang," Longarm said.

"Hang!" the outlaw yelped, twisting his head to try to look up at Longarm. "I never did anything to hang for!"

Longarm hunkered on his heels next to the man and took out a cheroot from his vest pocket. He clamped his teeth down on the unlit smoke and said around it, "What do you call murderin' a deputy United States marshal?"

The wounded man rolled his eyes at Longarm like a spooked horse. "I didn't shoot him! It was Horne that done it, and you know that!"

"'S funny," Longarm said. "I reckon I'm the only real witness, and I sorta disremember exactly what happened. I'm thinkin' maybe it was you who pulled the trigger, mister."

The outlaw let out a groan of despair. "This ain't right!

I done some robberies, and you can send me to prison for that, I reckon, but I never killed nobody! Not ever! I swear it, mister, whoever you are."

Longarm rolled the cheroot to the other side of his mouth. "Deputy U.S. Marshal Custis Long. A jury's gonna believe whatever I tell 'em, old son, so you better do some hard thinkin', startin' right now. Where were Horne and the rest of your bunch headed from El Paso?"

"I . . . I don't know. The whole gang was gonna split up, I swear it. Horne said things would be too hot for a while for us to stay together."

"After you divvied up the loot, you mean?"

The outlaw shook his head. "We weren't gonna divide the loot now."

Longarm frowned and asked, "What in blazes do you mean by that?"

"Horne convinced us it'd be too dangerous to split up the money now. He said the law would be on the lookout for the bills and it'd be better for us to wait awhile. So he stashed it somewhere and we were gonna get back together here in El Paso in six months to divvy it."

Longarm took the cheroot from his mouth and thought for a moment. Then he said, "You realize Horne was gonna double-cross you, don't you?"

"He wouldn't do that. We were all partners. Anyway, he had to know that if he tried somethin' like that, the rest of us would hunt him down and kill him, even if we never saw a penny of that loot."

Longarm wasn't convinced, but Horne had been able to persuade his partners in crime that he was telling the truth, and that was all that mattered.

Now Horne was on one side of the border and the rest of the gang was on the other, at least for the time being. Horne might regard that as a lucky break. He could fade out of sight with his knowledge of where the stolen money was hidden, and the other outlaws wouldn't have any idea where he had gone. With El Paso in an uproar over the shoot-out at Mama Lupe's and the killing of Deputy U.S. Marshal Bert Collins, they wouldn't dare slip back across the river to try to pick up Horne's trail either, at least not for a while.

That would give Longarm a chance to track down Gideon Horne and arrest him. He would have to do his best not to kill the bastard, he reminded himself, otherwise the hidden loot might never be recovered.

"Marshal," the wounded outlaw whined, "Marshal, I really need a doctor. My leg hurts like blazes where you plugged me."

"You're a lucky man to hurt like that," Longarm told him.

"Lucky? How do you figure?"

Longarm looked at the body of Bert Collins, lying facedown in a pool of dark red blood, and said in a bleak voice, "The dead don't feel a damn thing."

Chapter 3

The doctor arrived a few minutes later to clean and bandage the wounded outlaw's leg. He proclaimed that the man was in no danger of dying from the wound unless he developed blood poisoning, which was unlikely.

"He'll live to hang," the medico said cheerfully. That sent another shiver through the wounded man.

"Like the old hymn tells us, further along we'll know more about it," said Longarm as he glared down at the outlaw. "For now, Benton, I reckon the sheriff won't mind lockin' this varmint up in his jail?"

Benton nodded. "We'll be glad to take care of that, Marshal, and hold him for as long as you need us to." He gestured toward the dead owlhoots. "We'll get these worthless sons of bitches planted, too, although there's a part of me that'd like to just toss 'em in the Rio because of what happened to Bert. No sense in fouling the river, though."

With everything under control now at Mama Lupe's, Longarm said, "Let's go see if we can find out anything about Horne." He paused on the way out to speak to the massive proprietor. "Sorry about all the bullet holes in the walls and the blood on the floor, Lupe."

The man shrugged his bull-like shoulders. "These things happen, Marshal," he said. "I'm sorry about Marshal Collins."

"Thanks." Longarm nodded and went out with Benton.

They walked quickly to the nearest of the bridges that spanned the Rio Grande. Four men holding rifles stood at the U.S. end of the bridge.

"Any sign of Horne?" Benton asked them.

One of the men shook his head. "He hasn't gotten across here, Fred. We've got the bridge shut down right now, nobody comin' or goin'."

"Good job," Benton said. "Keep it that way until you hear different."

He and Longarm walked downstream to the second bridge, where they found the same situation. The armed guards there swore that no one had crossed over into Mexico.

Longarm frowned in thought as he tugged at his right earlobe, then scraped his thumbnail along the line of his jaw. "Horne might've been able to circle around and get to one of the bridges before those deputies closed 'em off," he said. "It ain't likely, but it ain't impossible."

"He's still somewhere here in El Paso," Benton declared. "I can feel it in my bones."

"I hope your bones are right. I need to rent a horse so I can start lookin' around town."

"You can use one of our mounts while you're here. I'll help you look, too. I know most of the places around here where a fugitive might go to ground."

"I'm obliged for that," said Longarm. "I know El Paso pretty well, but I reckon you know it better."

The two men spent the night searching the border

town, checking at every saloon, whorehouse, cantina, gambling den, and shady flophouse. They saw plenty of squalor and vice, but no sign of Gideon Horne.

None of the bartenders, soiled doves, tinhorns, and grifters they talked to would admit to seeing anyone who matched the outlaw's description either. Benton seemed convinced that they were telling the truth.

"They know how hard on them we can make it if we want to," he said. "The more they cooperate, the less chance we'll bother them in the future."

Longarm wasn't sure about that, though he had no choice but to accept the local lawman's judgment in the matter.

The sun wasn't up yet as Longarm and Benton rode back to the sheriff's office, but it was close enough to the horizon so that the craggy peak of Mount Franklin just north of the town was already painted with splashes of orange and gold. Longarm was tired, but the memory of Bert Collins's bullet-riddled body drove him on.

"Has there been a train through here since the one I came in on last night?" he asked Benton. "We should've posted somebody at the depot."

Benton shook his head. "No trains. But there's one due in about twenty minutes, an eastbound. I'll get some men down to the station to make sure nobody who gets on it is Horne."

"Thanks. Of course, there was nothing stopping him from circlin' back around once he got out of town and crossin' the river into Mexico either upstream or downstream."

"Except it would be hard to ford right now," Benton reminded him. "And it's to Horne's advantage to stay on this side of the Rio, where the rest of his gang can't get at him."

Longarm grunted. "You thought of that, too, huh?

Things couldn't have worked out better for Horne if he wanted to pull a double-cross on his men. I know that varmint I winged said Horne wouldn't do that, but I wouldn't put anything past an owlhoot like him."

"Me neither," Benton agreed. "You want some breakfast?"

"After the night we've had, that sounds mighty good," Longarm said.

"I know just the place."

They put the horses in the stable behind the county courthouse that the sheriff's deputies used for their mounts. Then Benton led Longarm a couple of blocks down the street to a little café run by a bosomy Mexican woman and her husband.

Several cups of the woman's strong coffee boosted Longarm's spirits, and a handful of tortillas rolled up and stuffed with steak, eggs, and chili peppers fueled his weary body and made him feel halfway human again.

While they were eating, one of the other deputies came in and headed for their table. "Figured I'd find you and the marshal here, Fred," he said.

The rawboned Benton had thumbed his hat back on his balding head. He nodded toward one of the empty chairs and told the newcomer, "Sit down, Royal. Have a cup of coffee and something to eat with us."

Royal shook his head. "I didn't come for breakfast. I got news about Horne."

Longarm had been taking a sip of coffee. He set his cup aside and leaned forward in his chair. "What sort of news?"

"He was spotted about an hour ago over in New Mexico Territory, heading northwest toward Las Cruces."

"Who spotted him?" asked Longarm.

"A farmer bringing a wagonload of vegetables into

town. Said a fella rode past him just before sunup like the Devil himself was after him."

"That could've been anybody," Benton said.

"Yeah, but this farmer stopped at a cantina for some breakfast and probably a drink that he won't mention to his wife when he gets home. He heard some folks in there talking about the ruckus at Mama Lupe's last night and how we've been looking for an hombre with a white streak in his hair." Royal gestured toward his own head. "The farmer said the fella who rode past him didn't have a hat on, and he looked a little like a skunk because of a white streak runnin' through his hair."

Longarm felt his heart slug a little heavier in his chest. He figured nobody else matching Gideon Horne's description would be riding hell-bent-for-leather out of El Paso at dawn.

"Horne laid low for a while," Longarm said, "and now he's makin' a run for it."

Benton nodded. "I got to admit, it sure sounds like him. What are you gonna do, Marshal?"

Longarm gave the only answer he could.

"Go after him."

The shots came out of the night with no warning, but Longarm wasn't really surprised. He'd been expecting an ambush. He went out of the saddle in a rolling dive a split-second after a bullet whipped past his ear.

He'd been riding with his Winchester in his right hand, the reins in his left. Holding tightly to the rifle as he hit the ground, he rolled over and came up on one knee.

The spot where the muzzle flashes had come from was etched in his brain. He brought the Winchester to his shoulder and cranked off three rounds as fast as he could work the weapon's lever.

He aimed all around the place where he'd seen gun flame bloom in the darkness, in the hope that no matter which way the bushwhacker had ducked, he would tag the son of a bitch.

The swift, sudden rataplan of hoofbeats told him that wasn't the case. The man who'd taken those potshots at him had a horse ready, and now, the ambush having failed, he was taking off again for the tall and uncut.

Longarm bit back a curse and aimed more shots at the sounds of the hoofbeats. It almost amounted to firing blind, and he didn't really expect to hit anything.

Sure enough, the horse didn't slow or even break stride. The hoofbeats continued their steady drumming. Longarm stopped wasting lead and just listened in disgust until the sounds had faded away completely.

"Horne, you bastard," Longarm said out loud, knowing that his quarry couldn't hear him but not really caring. "I'll get you sooner or later, old son. You can't run far enough to lose me."

He hoped that wasn't just false bravado intended to prop up his own spirits. Longarm really did believe that he would catch up to every owlhoot he set out after, and during his long career as a deputy United States marshal, he had been right a lot more often than not.

He didn't want a murdering son of a bitch like Gideon Horne to ruin that record.

With a sigh, Longarm stood up and looked around for his horse. There was no moon, but the millions of stars provided enough light for him to spot the animal standing on a rocky little hummock about a hundred yards away. It had spooked and bolted when the shooting started.

That was one of the drawbacks of having to use rented mounts and horses that he requisitioned from army posts. He never really got to know the horses he was riding, never had a chance to learn how they would react in certain situations.

Sometimes he thought he ought to find himself a good horse and stick with it, but with the sort of life he led, always at the beck and call of Uncle Sam, that wasn't really practical.

Sort of like with women, he supposed.

He began trudging toward the horse. The sandy, gravelly ground tugged at his boots and made walking difficult.

During his younger years, he had cowboyed enough to become a firm believer in the idea that any job worth doing ought to be done from horseback. He'd never liked walking all that much. Worse still was walking in a desert, which this area almost was.

Not quite, though. The real desert was still a number of miles to the north, the direction Gideon Horne had been heading after the failed ambush.

The real desert was called Death Valley.

The big lawman was about ten yards from the horse when the animal decided to spook again. It turned and trotted off without looking back.

Longarm wanted to yell curses after it, but that might just make the horse run away even harder. He settled for muttering, "Damn fool jughead," under his breath.

He turned to his right, hoping to circle around and get ahead of the horse. He'd rented the animal in Las Vegas, to replace the played-out mount he had rented in Flagstaff, which had replaced the one he'd rented down in Phoenix . . .

The series of horses stretched back a couple of weeks and several hundred miles to El Paso, where Longarm had picked up an army mount from the post at Fort Bliss before setting off after Gideon Horne.

Since then it had been a long, hard, frustrating chase

as Longarm tried to run the outlaw to ground. He was
dressed in range clothes now, rather than the tweed suit
that the President's lady favored.

Longarm was still convinced that Horne had intended
to give the law the slip, circle back around, pick up the
loot, and all of it would be his alone.

But until now, Longarm had been dogging his trail so
closely that Horne hadn't had a chance to carry out that
plan. The chase had stretched through New Mexico and
Arizona and now on across the southern tip of Nevada
and into California.

A couple of times, Longarm had almost caught up
with his quarry, but somehow Horne had slipped away at
the last moment. Horne had set up several ambushes for
his pursuer, but each time Longarm had dodged the bullets, literally, including tonight.

Longarm didn't know how Horne felt about it, but he
thought this chase was getting damned wearisome.

"You ain't gettin' away from me, old son," he said
now as he plodded after the skittish horse. "I'll shoot
you before I let you run off and leave me out here in the
middle of nowhere."

He wouldn't do that, of course. He wasn't the sort of
man to hurt a dumb animal, let alone shoot one down in
cold blood.

At the moment, though, he sure as hell felt like doing
it, and a minute later the impulse became even stronger
as the horse suddenly let out a whinny and broke into a
gallop.

Longarm bit back a curse and started running after it,
but of course he stood no chance of catching up to the
runaway, and he knew it.

After a minute or so, he stopped and stared bleakly at
the dwindling plume of dust in the distance. That was all

he could see of the horse, and soon that was gone, too, along with the sound of hoofbeats.

He was alone and afoot, a hell of a long way from anywhere.

And with every passing moment, Gideon Horne was getting farther away from him.

Chapter 4

Without any way to catch the horse, Longarm continued trudging northward. That was the way Horne had gone, and no matter how bad things looked right now, Longarm wasn't going to give up on catching the outlaw.

He knew that if he did that, he wouldn't be able to banish the memory of Bert Collins's bloody corpse lying on the floor of Mama Lupe's.

It was still possible the horse might stop somewhere up ahead. Since it was too hot in these parts to walk much during the day, even at this time of year, Longarm knew he had to take advantage of the darkness and put as much ground behind him as he could while the blistering sun wasn't blasting down on him.

When it started to get light, he could hunt some shade and find a place to rest during the worst of the heat.

The air held a distinct chill at night, as desert air always does. Longarm tried to ignore it, along with the thirst that already dried out his mouth.

Water was scarce around here, and some of it that he might come across wouldn't be fit to drink because of the alkali and other minerals in it. His best bet would be to find a hole with some rainwater caught in it.

Assuming, of course, that it had rained in a month of Sundays, which in this part of California was a risky assumption.

Longarm put one foot in front of the other and tried not to think about the cold, or how dry his mouth was, or how Gideon Horne was getting away.

There were some little mining towns up around Death Valley, he recalled, and he could probably walk to one of them in a day or two.

But by then Horne would have a big lead on him, maybe too big a lead for Longarm to overcome. That knowledge put a bitter, sour taste under the big lawman's tongue.

After what seemed like a year, the eastern sky turned rosy with the approach of dawn. The sun rose swiftly, and it wasn't long before the giant orange orb was peeking over the horizon.

Longarm found a cluster of boulders. They wouldn't give him much shade, and he would have to move during the day as the sun moved to stay out of its fierce glare, but the place was better than nothing.

As he stretched out in the shelter of one of the rocks, he started digging in the sandy soil with his hand. It was possible that if he dug down far enough, he might find a tiny trickle of muddy water seeping into the hole.

Exhaustion claimed him before that could happen. His eyes closed, and he slept.

The heat woke him later. The sun beat down on him until he crawled into the shade of another rock.

He didn't have enough energy to try digging again. He just went back to sleep instead.

When he woke a second time, he realized that he was in danger. Even though he hadn't been without food and water all that long, the desert sapped a man's strength in a hurry. Weakened as he was, he knew that if he went back to sleep, he might not wake up when the sun touched him again.

He might simply lie there and let it bake him to death.

The idea of being a fresh-baked corpse brought a grim chuckle to Longarm's lips. He sat up, propping his back against the rock that shaded him.

The rock wasn't very cool, but at least it wasn't as hot as the burning sands that stretched out in all directions around the clump of boulders. He didn't know how they had come to crop up in this particular place in the arid landscape, but they were going to save his life.

Despite his best intentions, he fell asleep again anyway. Time passed, and when he awoke again, it was dusk. He had slept the day away. He was sitting there yawning and rubbing at his eyes when he heard a crunching sound.

It seemed to be coming from behind the rock where he was. Slowly and clumsily because he was so weak, he pulled himself up and turned to look back over the low boulder.

At first he thought he was delirious from thirst. Then he realized that his eyes weren't playing tricks on him after all.

This area didn't have much vegetation in it. The climate was too arid for that.

But a few clumps of hardy grass sprouted here and there, and one such clump was about fifty yards away from the rocks.

The horse that had run away the night before stood next to that grass, calmly cropping on it. That was what Longarm had heard.

Longarm's first impulse was to break into a stumbling run toward the horse and try to grab the canteen off the saddle. It took every bit of his self-control to stifle that urge.

Instead, he waited, letting the horse graze and hoping that would settle the animal's jangled nerves. If it ran off again, that might well be a death sentence for the big lawman.

Being patient seemed to work, hard though it was, because the horse didn't shy away when Longarm finally left the rocks and sidled closer. He talked softly as his boots crunched on the sandy soil.

A few yards separated him from the animal, then only a few more feet. The horse was right there, with the canteen hanging tantalizingly from the saddle . . .

"Got you," Longarm husked through cracked, paper-dry lips as he reached out and grasped the dangling reins. The horse just raised its head and gave him a look as if to ask, *Where did you think I was going?*

Longarm slid the Winchester back into the sheath strapped to the saddle. He patted the horse's shoulder and murmured to it, calming it even more.

Then he untied the strap holding the canteen to the saddle. Water sloshed enticingly inside as he pulled the cork.

His hand trembled a little as he raised the canteen. He moistened his lips first, fighting the urge to guzzle down every drop. Then he took a sip, waited a few moments, took another.

The liquid didn't quench his thirst because his body soaked it up so quickly, but it was a start anyway. The last thing he wanted to do was drink all the water and have his stomach rebel and throw it back up.

Longarm carried some jerky in the saddlebags. He fished out a piece and put it in his mouth. He started to chew, slowly softening the strip of tough, dried meat.

Strength began to ooze back into his muscles from

the savory juices. When he finished the jerky, he took another sip of water.

He was going to live, he told himself.

And more than that, he was going to catch up to Gideon Horne and bring the outlaw to justice.

Even though Horne's ambush had failed, circumstances had come close to killing Longarm anyway. But they hadn't, and sooner or later Horne would find out just what a stroke of bad luck that had been for him.

Night had fallen by the time Longarm put his foot in the stirrup and swung up into the saddle. He felt considerably stronger now, and he was no longer parched from thirst.

Now that he was higher, he noticed something that he hadn't been able to see before. A small scattering of lights winked and glimmered in the distance to the north.

Death Valley lay in that direction, and so did the mining town of Panamint, Longarm recalled. Would Horne head for the settlement, or would he try to avoid it?

So far, Horne hadn't shied away from towns. They were few and far between out here, and a man had to have supplies, even though it meant leaving a trail behind him of witnesses who could say that he'd been there.

Las Vegas was several days behind the outlaw and his pursuer. Longarm thought there was a good chance Horne had seen those lights in the distance the night before and headed for Panamint.

Because of that, Longarm turned the horse in that direction and heeled the animal into a lope.

His previous visits to Panamint hadn't left him all that impressed with the place. It had been in existence only for a few years, springing to life when gold, silver, and copper deposits had been discovered in the hills around Death Valley.

The valley itself, with its miles and miles of sand and empty salt flats, wasn't much good for anything, although some folks had started talking about trying to mine something called borax from them.

Numerous mines producing the more valuable minerals were located in the Panamint Mountains to the west and the Amargosa Range to the east, as well as in the foothills along the edges of the valley.

Settlements like Panamint and Ballarat served as supply points for those mines, as well as for the hundreds of diehard prospectors who roamed Death Valley and its environs, still searching for strikes of their own.

Panamint provided more than supplies, Longarm recalled. It also provided entertainment, in the form of liquor, gambling, and women, for the men who labored in the mines. It was a wide-open town, with no real law, or at least it was that way the last time Longarm had visited the settlement.

So if he caught up to Gideon Horne there, he knew he couldn't count on any help from a local badge toter, because there might not be one.

That was all right with Longarm. He had worked alone for most of his career and liked it that way.

When you didn't have a partner, you didn't have to worry about said partner getting stabbed, shot in the back, or otherwise killed. You could look out for your own hide, which Longarm did with remarkable proficiency.

Bert Collins's death had brought that home to Longarm, and it was a lesson he didn't expect to forget anytime soon.

The lights were a lot farther away than they appeared to be at first glance, of course. Having traveled a lot in the desert, Longarm expected that.

It took him several hours to reach the settlement.

Along the way, he rode through a long valley formed by rugged ridges that bulked darkly and menacingly on either side of him. Surprise Valley, he thought it was called. He kept his eyes on the lights and let them guide him.

He knew it had to be after midnight when he finally rode into Panamint's deserted main street, which stretched for nearly a mile in front of him. He didn't bother fishing out his big turnip watch to check.

Instead, he turned the horse toward the nearest saloon, thinking that he would ask there if anybody had seen a stranger matching Horne's description.

He hadn't reached the saloon when a man suddenly stepped out of the shadows, swung up a shotgun, and said, "Hold it right there, mister, or I'll blow you out of that saddle."

Longarm had been threatened many times before, and he knew how to judge the danger and react accordingly. This hombre sounded nervous, which meant a couple of things.

He didn't *want* to shoot Longarm.

But he might be more likely to do it anyway, simply because he was spooked.

At this range, a double load of buckshot would make hash out of him, Longarm knew, so he reined in carefully.

"Take it easy, old son," he said in a calm, controlled voice as he slowly lifted his hands, keeping them in sight at all times and not making any fast moves. "I ain't lookin' for trouble."

"Then what *are* you lookin' for?"

Longarm played a hunch and decided it might be best to keep his real identity a secret for now. The leather folder containing his badge and identification papers was tucked away safely in his saddlebags. For the time being, he would leave it there.

He nodded toward the saloon which had been his destination and said, "Thought I'd get a drink."

The barrels of the Greener didn't waver. "You ain't lookin' for anybody in particular?"

"Who would I be lookin' for? I hate to tell you this, friend, but I don't reckon I know a soul in this fine town of yours."

Finally, the man lowered the shotgun a little. Longarm could see him well enough in the light that came from the buildings to tell that he was a tall, lanky hombre in well-worn work clothes and a felt hat with a wide, floppy brim. Longarm figured him for a miner or a prospector, or maybe a teamster.

"All right, I reckon you can go get your drink—" he began.

"Tim, who's that with you?"

The voice that interrupted the man belonged to a woman. Longarm turned his head and saw her striding briskly toward them, holding her skirts up a little to keep them from dragging in the dusty street.

He couldn't tell much about her except that she seemed to be average height for a woman, and she moved like she was relatively young. It appeared that she had come from a nearby house with a small, fenced yard in front of it. The gate was open. Not much would grow around here, but a woman might have a cactus garden or something in a yard like that.

The man with the shotgun, whose name evidently was Tim, turned and lowered the weapon the rest of the way so that the barrels pointed at the ground. He tucked the Greener under one arm and used the other hand to yank his hat off.

With a respectful nod, he said, "Just a fella passin' through town who wants a drink, Miss Amelia."

The woman came closer and stopped to look up at

Longarm. She wore a white blouse that came up to her neck. Dark hair was piled on top of her head. Longarm still couldn't make out her features, but her voice was a pleasant contralto as she spoke again.

What she said wasn't all that pleasant, though. She looked up at Longarm and declared, "Well, he can't stop for a drink, and you know it, Tim." Her chin jutted defiantly as she went on, "I'm sorry, sir, but you're going to have to turn that horse around and ride out of Panamint, right now."

Chapter 5

The unexpected command, as well as the stern tone of the woman's voice, brought a frown of puzzlement to Longarm's face. He had a job to do here, and he didn't intend to be ordered out of town by anybody, even a woman.

He reached up, touched his hat brim, and gave her the same sort of respectful nod Tim had. Then he said, "Sorry, ma'am, but I can't do that."

"Why not?" she asked.

"Like I told this hombre, I'd like a drink. I've been on the trail for quite a spell. Need to wet my whistle."

"Then ride over to Ballarat. It's not that far from here. You can get a drink there."

It was possible that Gideon Horne had gone to Ballarat, but Panamint was in a direct line with the way he'd been riding. Longarm thought it was a lot more likely he would pick up the outlaw's trail here.

"Yes, ma'am, I suppose I could, but I'm here now, and it's dark, and I don't see no reason why I should."

Longarm shifted in the saddle, getting ready to swing down from the horse's back.

"Tim! Stop him!"

At the sharply voiced command, the man stepped back and started to lift the shotgun again.

Longarm lost patience then. He slid his right foot from the stirrup and kicked out with it.

The toe of his boot struck the shotgun's breech and sent the weapon flying out of the man's hands. Tim yelped in pain and surprise as he jumped back.

Longarm palmed out his Colt. He didn't point the revolver at either Tim or the woman, but he held it ready in case he needed it.

"Both of you settle down," he told them. "This sure ain't a very friendly town."

"You're making a big mistake," the woman told him in clipped tones. "You don't know how big."

"If that's true, it won't be the first time I've fouled up. Meanwhile, I'm gonna get that drink."

He dismounted then, still holding his gun and keeping an eye on Tim in case the man made a lunge for the scattergun.

Tim just stood there, though, looking angry and confused. He shot several glances toward the woman as if waiting for her to tell him what to do.

She didn't issue any more orders. She just glared at Longarm and said, "All right, it's your own choice. Whatever happens to you, it's on your own head, Mister . . . ?"

"Parker," Longarm said, supplying the alias he often used when he didn't want folks to know that he was a lawman. "Custis Parker. Why do you want to know?" He grinned. "In case the undertaker needs it for the tombstone?"

"Exactly," the woman said.

Then she turned and walked back toward the house she had come from. Her back was stiff with anger.

Longarm frowned after her and said to Tim, "A mite bossy, ain't she?"

"She's got a right to be. She's the only sawbones in these parts."

Longarm looked over at the man. "That lady's a doctor?"

"Yep. Dr. Amelia Judd."

In his travels, Longarm had run across female physicians several times. He recalled one in particular over in the Ozark Mountains of Arkansas.

He hadn't really expected to find a lady doctor in a wild and woolly mining town like Panamint, though.

"Why was she so dead set on me gettin' out of town?" he asked Tim.

"You'd have to ask her about that," the man replied in a surly voice. "All right if I get my shotgun now?"

Longarm nodded toward the double-barreled weapon. "Go ahead. But don't get any funny ideas in your head, old son." He hefted the .44. "I'm ready for trouble now."

"No trouble," Tim said as he picked up the Greener. "Miss Amelia told you what you ought to do. If you don't, it ain't on anybody's head but yours."

He walked away. With another puzzled frown on his face, Longarm watched Tim go.

They were the only current citizens of Panamint he had met so far, and if they were any indication, the whole town had gone loco.

But maybe they were the exceptions to the rule, he told himself. He pouched his iron and walked toward the saloon he had noticed earlier, leading the horse.

The place was called the Copper Queen, no doubt after one of the valuable minerals found in the area. The lamps were lit, casting a yellow glow through the windows, and as Longarm approached, he expected to hear music and laughter coming from inside.

Instead, it was quiet, even though the doors were open. The batwings across the entrance weren't enough to muffle any noise. Longarm's frown deepened as he looped the horse's reins around the hitch rail and stepped up onto the boardwalk in front of the saloon.

He was tall enough so that he could look over the batwings and peer into the Copper Queen. A number of men stood at the bar, nursing the drinks they had in front of them.

Every one of the hombres wore a glum expression, as if he had just come from a funeral . . . or was about to attend one. Nobody said anything.

Longarm couldn't figure out what had put the whole town into mourning. Maybe all the mines had petered out, he thought. Maybe Panamint was on its last legs.

A woman came into Longarm's view, moving across the room from his left to his right as she walked toward the bar. She wore a low-cut, dark green gown that went well with her creamy skin and the auburn curls that tumbled down onto her mostly bare shoulders.

She was beautiful, but she wore the same sort of solemn expression as the men in the room. She came up to the bar, rested a hand on the hardwood, and said, "I think we'll go ahead and close down for the night, Clancy."

The bartender was big, with a craggy, battered face and gray hair. He looked like he might have done some prizefighting in his time.

"Aye, Miss Dallas," he rumbled. "I don't think any of these lads will complain."

The hard look he cast toward the drinkers made sure that they wouldn't.

Longarm figured that if he wanted to wet his whistle— and get any information about Gideon Horne tonight—

he'd better go ahead and get in there. He pushed the
batwings aside and stepped into the Copper Queen.

The woman turned to look at him. "We're just about
to close up, mister—" she began.

She stopped short and studied him more closely. Longarm saw frank appraisal in her green eyes. He thought he
saw approval there, too.

But there was something else present in her gaze:
surprise.

She must have expected to see one of the locals, not a
stranger.

She took a step toward him and said, "You're not from
around here, are you, mister?"

"Nope," Longarm admitted. "Is it a rule that you have
to be from Panamint to get a drink in here?"

"No, of course not. I just . . . didn't expect to see
somebody new." She got over her surprise. "We're clos-
ing. Sorry."

"You can't stay open long enough for me to have one
drink?"

She shook her head. "No, I'm afraid not." She turned
to the bartender. "Clancy, put the cork in the bottle."

"Aye, lass."

The other men shuffled out past Longarm, leaving
only him, the redhead, and Clancy in the saloon. Longarm knew that Clancy's hostile, narrow-eyed gaze was
calculated to send him scurrying after the others.

Instead, he stood his ground and said, "You know,
Panamint strikes me as not a very friendly place. I've
only been here a few minutes, and already I've had a
shotgun pointed at me and two beautiful women have
told me to get out."

The redhead's chin came up. "What other woman are
you talking about?"

So she knew she was one of the beauties he referred to and accepted the compliment without question. That made Longarm like her. He didn't care for it when women put on an air of false modesty.

"Dr. Judd," he said.

She inclined her head to the side. "I'm not sure I'd go so far as to call her beautiful, but I suppose that depends on your taste. She told you to get out of town?"

"Yeah. Said I ought to head over to Ballarat." Longarm scraped his thumbnail along his jaw. "I'm the stubborn sort, though."

"One drink?"

He shrugged. "Yeah, that'd do me, I reckon."

He figured he could stretch it out into more than that, once he got started.

The redhead nodded to Clancy. "Pour it. And one for me, while you're at it."

Clancy frowned in obvious disapproval, but he uncorked a bottle and splashed whiskey into two glasses. He set the bottle on the bar and said, "I'll be goin' now, if ye don't mind, Miss Dallas."

"That's fine," she told him. "I'll lock up."

Clancy took off his apron, folded it and tossed it onto a shelf underneath the bar, and came out from behind the hardwood. Still glaring at Longarm, he shambled toward the door like a big Irish bear.

The redhead handed one of the glasses to Longarm and picked up the other for herself.

"My name is Dallas Farrar," she said.

"Custis Parker," Longarm supplied. "I get the feelin' you own this place, Miss Farrar."

"Call me Dallas. Everybody else in Panamint does. And yes, I own the Copper Queen."

"I figured it was named for the mineral. Now I'm wonderin' if it was named for that coppery hair of yours."

"Take your pick," she said. "I don't suppose it really matters." She lifted her glass and laughed. "Here's to your health, Custis."

Something about the way she said it, along with a brittle edge that crept into her laugh, warned Longarm. He thought for a second the whiskey might be drugged.

But she threw her drink back without hesitation, and Longarm had seen Clancy fill both glasses from the same bottle. He downed the whiskey.

It wasn't the best he'd ever tasted, but it wasn't bad. And there didn't seem to be anything wrong with it.

Dallas set her glass on the bar. "All right, you've had that one drink. Are you leaving now?"

"The saloon, or the settlement?"

Creamy shoulders rose and fell. "Take your pick."

"I'd just as soon not do either," said Longarm. He slid his empty glass across the hardwood. "What I'd like is another drink."

"You said one."

"People say a lot of things."

Dallas laughed again, and it didn't sound quite so brittle this time. "That they do," she agreed. She picked up the bottle and poured, refilling both glasses. "I have a hunch there's more to you than what you say, Custis. You're awfully stubborn for a man who's just passing through."

"Well, to tell you the truth, I'm supposed to meet a fella here in Panamint."

"Is that so?"

"Yeah. Sort of a big, good-lookin' hombre."

Dallas ran her green eyes over his rangy frame. "That could describe a lot of people."

"Oh, you'd know this fella if you saw him. He's got dark hair, but there's a white streak in it. You can't miss it."

Even as he spoke, he saw something flare in her eyes. She knew who he was talking about. Longarm was sure about that.

The question was whether Gideon Horne was still here in Panamint or had moved on already.

If he was still here, Longarm vowed not to let him get away again.

Dallas shook her head and said, "Sorry. I don't recall seeing anybody who looks like that. And the Copper Queen is the best saloon in town. Just about everybody who comes to Panamint stops in here sooner or later."

"I don't doubt it," Longarm replied, although he did doubt that she was telling the truth about seeing Horne. "But it's mighty important that I talk to this fella. Maybe I'll ask around town about him."

"It won't do you any good," Dallas said quickly. "Maybe you should do like Dr. Judd told you and ride on over to Ballarat. Your friend could be there."

"Never said he was my friend," drawled Longarm. "Just that it's important I talk to him."

"Well, whatever it is you want with him, he's not here." Dallas swallowed her second shot of whiskey. "Drink up, Custis, and then you can get going."

Longarm set his glass on the bar without emptying it. "This is just about the unfriendliest town I ever did see."

"So you think we're unfriendly, do you?"

"Ever since I rode in, folks have been tryin' to get me to leave."

Dallas's eyes flashed as if she had just reached a decision. "I'll show you how unfriendly we are," she said as she stepped closer to Longarm. She took hold of his arms and came up on her toes.

Then her full red lips were pressed hotly to his mouth in an urgent kiss that sent lightning bolts of pleasure crackling through Longarm's body.

Chapter 6

The same war that had been fought many times within Longarm was fought again now.

He had come to Panamint to find Gideon Horne, not to dally with a beautiful redhead. Which emotion would rule him, the desire he felt for Dallas Farrar or the sense of duty and justice that had always been with him?

Maybe both, he thought.

Dallas knew more than she was telling. The instincts that had served him so well over the years made him certain of that.

She might be more likely to reveal what she knew if he played along with her . . . or this sudden passion for him she exhibited could be a sham, the bait for some sort of trap.

Either way, he might find out what he wanted to know.

So he returned the kiss, matching passion for passion. His tongue prodded eagerly against her lips, which opened to allow him to explore the warm, wet cavern of her mouth. She met his probing tongue with her own, which swirled around his in a sensuous dance.

Dallas slid her hands up his arms until she could reach

around his neck. At the same time, he put his arms around her waist and drew her hard against him, molding her body to his own. Her flesh was warm and yielding under the green gown.

Longarm felt her breasts flatten against his chest. Even through both sets of clothes, he felt her nipples hardening until they were like sharp pebbles poking into him.

His cock was growing hard, too, and she had to be aware of the long, thick shaft pressing against the softness of her belly. She proved that by moaning deep in her throat as she ground herself into him.

It was a long, heated kiss, but Dallas finally drew back and whispered, "My room is upstairs. You'll come up there with me, Custis?"

"You don't really think there's any chance I'd say no, do you?" he asked with a grin.

Dallas laughed. "No, not really." She took hold of his hand. "Come on."

Longarm jerked his head toward the front doors. "Don't you reckon you'd better lock up first? Otherwise some varmint's liable to come in and start helpin' himself to your liquor."

"I don't think we have to worry about that. As late as it is, everybody will be staying pretty close to home for the rest of the night."

"Maybe, but I'd hate to be responsible for your place gettin' robbed."

He would hate even more making it easy for someone to sneak into the saloon and ambush him while Dallas distracted him. He didn't believe that was what was going on here, but it never hurt anything to be careful.

A look of mild annoyance sparked in her green eyes. "All right," she said. "I'll lock up. Why don't you grab that bottle and the glasses, and we'll take them with us?"

Longarm did as she suggested, tossing back the second drink she'd poured before he picked up the bottle and the other glass.

While he was doing that, she went to the doors, closed them, and fished a key out of a pocket in her gown. She twisted the key in the lock.

"I'll blow out some of the lamps, too," she said as she pocketed the key and came back toward the bar.

Longarm helped her with that. They left only one lamp burning behind the bar, and the wick was turned down low on it.

Dallas led him upstairs to a hallway that was dimly lit by a lamp at the far end. She opened a door that wasn't locked and took him into a large, comfortable-looking bedroom that was situated at a corner of the building so that it had cross-ventilation from two windows.

This close to Death Valley, it was warm enough all the time so that catching whatever vagrant breezes there might be was a good idea.

Dallas lit a lamp on a small table beside a four-poster that dominated the room. A dressing table on the opposite side of the room had a large mirror attached to it, Longarm noted, which might lead to some interesting observations at times.

The walls were covered with light yellow wallpaper dotted with tiny flowers. Thick drapes over the windows were a slightly darker shade of yellow. They were open a little, but Dallas immediately drew them closed.

A signal? Not necessarily, but Longarm wondered about that anyway.

If this was a trap, it wouldn't be the first time a beautiful woman had used her body in such a way against him. He would just be prepared for anything that happened, he told himself.

He wasn't quite prepared, though, for the sheer beauty of Dallas's breasts when she revealed them by reaching behind her back and doing something to the dress that made it spill forward and gather around her waist.

Her breasts were full, firm globes of flesh crowned by large, dark red nipples that stood out a good half an inch, maybe a little more. She reached up and caressed them as she smiled at Longarm.

"You can see how excited you've gotten me, Custis," she said. She looked down at his groin. "And I can see how excited I'm getting you."

That was the damned truth, he thought. His shaft was rock-hard, or close to it anyway. Hard enough that it was sure as hell getting a mite uncomfortable being confined in his trousers that way. A throb of anticipation went through it as Dallas sashayed toward him and reached for the buttons of his fly.

She unfastened them deftly while he was unbuckling his gun belt. He coiled the belt and held it and the holstered Colt while she unbuckled his other belt.

She pulled his shirttails out, hooked her fingers in the waistband of the trousers and the long underwear he wore underneath them, and dragged the whole shooting match down over his hips.

That allowed his cock to spring free, which it did eagerly, the head bobbing a little as the thick shaft jutted out from the nest of dark hair at his groin.

"Why, Custis," Dallas said, and she sounded genuinely impressed rather than calculatingly coy. "That's even more than I expected."

"Not too much, I hope," Longarm said.

"Oh, no," she murmured. "Never too much."

He turned and set the gun belt on a chair beside the bed, where it would be within fairly easy reach if he needed it.

When he turned back toward her, he found that she had pushed the gown and her underthings down over her hips so that the garments puddled on the floor around her feet. Naked except for stockings and high-buttoned shoes, she stepped out of the clothes and dropped to her knees in front of him.

She wrapped her hands around his manhood and held it steady so that she could nuzzle her cheek against the head. Her touch was hot and made him throb again. She made a small sound of satisfaction as she felt his cock pulse against her skin.

Her tongue came out and licked around the head. Then it traced a fiery path along the length of the shaft to his balls. She cupped them in her hand and rolled them back and forth as she worked her tongue back up the other side to the head.

"Take your shirt off," she whispered.

Quickly, Longarm unbuttoned the shirt and peeled it off his muscular torso. As he tossed it aside, he realized that he was still wearing his boots and his hat. He had to look a mite ridiculous, and a guffaw almost burst from him as he thought about how he must look.

What Dallas was doing to him with her lips and tongue was mighty serious business, though, so he didn't laugh. He just took the hat off and threw it aside, too, then tangled his fingers in her thick red hair and held on for dear life as her head began to bob up and down on him.

That was one exceptional French lesson she gave him, and Longarm came damn close a couple of times to rewarding her with a mouthful of scalding juices.

He restrained the impulses, telling himself that he wanted Dallas to be good and satisfied so that she would be more likely to tell him what he wanted to know when this was all over.

That was as good a reason as any, he thought.

He caught hold of her soft, warm shoulders and lifted

her away from his cock, although he felt a pang of loss as her eager mouth left his flesh. Sweeping her up in his arms, he turned toward the bed and laid her down on the thick comforter that served as a spread.

"Custis," she said, her voice breathless, "you . . . you'll have to take your boots off."

Then as her legs opened and instinctively spread wide, he saw the moisture sparkling in the triangle of fine-spun, dark red hair where her thighs came together. She was already very wet.

"Oh, the hell with it!" she gasped. "Get that big thing inside me now!"

"Always glad to oblige a lady," he said in a voice made husky with need.

He stood at the edge of the bed, reached under her to grasp her buttocks, and pulled and lifted her so she was positioned perfectly for his thrust. He drove forward without aiming.

"Oh, God, don't miss!" Dallas cried. "You hit the wrong hole and you'll tear me apart!"

Longarm didn't miss. His shaft sank unerringly into her honeypot, burying itself to the hilt between the hot, buttery folds of flesh.

Dallas moaned, closed her eyes, and began to toss her head back and forth in ecstasy. Longarm had just penetrated her, but she was climaxing already despite that.

There was nothing phony about it either. She couldn't fake the rippling spasms that went through her body. Longarm felt her interior muscles clenching and unclenching on his shaft. He left it sheathed within her, not moving as her culmination washed over her.

After a moment, Dallas let out a soft little scream as she arched her back. She held it that way for a couple of heartbeats, then sighed and sagged back down onto the thick mattress. Her perfect breasts rose and fell quickly as she tried to catch her breath.

Eventually, her eyelids fluttered open. She looked up at him and said, "Custis, that was . . . that was amazing. I know, women say that all the time when they're with a man, but . . . but this time it's true. Oh, Lord, it's true . . ."

Her voice trailed off as her green eyes widened with amazement.

"Custis, you're not getting soft," she said.

"That's because I ain't done yet," he told her.

Then he tightened his grip on her thighs, pulled out slightly, and surged forward again, driving deep inside her.

His hips moved back and forth powerfully, like the pistons on a great steam engine. Dallas began to thrash her head from side to side again as a second, unexpected crescendo of excitement and lust welled up within her.

Longarm kept up the pace for several minutes as he felt his own climax building within him. When Dallas began to spasm again, he let go of the iron grip he had been keeping on his own reins and thrust into her as far as he could go. He shuddered and groaned as his juices began to spill into her.

Longarm emptied himself, filling her to overflowing. His pulse hammered inside his head as he let go. He managed to stay on his feet, but for a second, his muscles were as limp as dishrags.

If there was ever a perfect moment for an ambush, a persistent little voice in the back of his head told him, this was it, right here and now.

Nothing happened except for Dallas saying, "My God . . . Custis . . . my heart's going to . . . give out! I swear it must be . . . about to jump out of my chest!"

He smiled as he gazed down at her. "I reckon I . . . know what you mean," he told her. "Feel like I been . . . rode hard and put up wet."

She wiggled her hips, causing his member to move very pleasurably inside her. "No, that's me," she said. "I'm not sure I've ever been ridden so hard, and I *know* I've never been this wet."

Longarm chuckled. "Now, ain't you glad I didn't ride on over to Ballarat like everybody wanted me to?"

He saw a shadow pass across her eyes and knew that his question had caused her to remember whatever it was she was trying to conceal from him. He hoped he hadn't made a mistake by bringing the subject up again too soon.

Evidently he had, because she pulled away from him. He could have held her in place, but he let her go, not wanting to make the situation worse. His shaft was starting to soften now, and it slid out of her with a liquid whisper.

Longarm expected Dallas to be mad at him. He wouldn't have been surprised if she had cussed him and told him to get the hell out of her room.

But he wasn't expecting her to roll onto her side, put her hands over her face, and start sobbing loudly.

Which was exactly what she did.

Chapter 7

"Wait a minute," Longarm said desperately, feeling the same sort of frantic helplessness that most men did when confronted with a bawling woman. "Don't carry on so, darlin'. I didn't mean for what we did to upset you—"

"Oh, sh-shut up, you b-big lummox!" she exclaimed between sobs. "Why do you think I'm upset?" She sat up on the bed, her ruby-tipped breasts bouncing enticingly. "Because you fucked me? You idiot! I wanted you to fuck me! I wanted to be fucked like I've never been fucked before, because this may be the last . . . the last time . . ."

She crumpled, curling up on her side again and crying even louder than before.

The last time, Longarm thought. The last time for what?

The last time she would ever know the pleasure of bedding a man?

That didn't make any sense. If there was one thing Dallas Farrar ought to be able to do whenever she wanted to, as often as she wanted to, for a long, long time yet, it was to enjoy the company of a man in her bed.

The only reason Longarm could think of why she couldn't do that would be if she wasn't alive anymore.

A chill colder than any desert night traced an icy path along his spine as that thought went through his brain.

"Dallas, listen to me," he said quietly but urgently. "What in blazes is goin' on in this town?"

Her response was quick . . . too quick.

"Nothing. I don't know what you're talking about."

Longarm leaned over the bed, resting his fists on the mattress on either side of her. He knew it was a threatening position and didn't like trying to intimidate her, but every instinct in his body now told him that something was very wrong in Panamint.

"Folks have been tryin' to get me out of this town ever since I got here," he said. "I don't think it's just a matter of bein' unfriendly either. People who live in a boomtown usually *want* more hombres comin' in."

Dallas looked up at him with wet eyes and shook her head. "You're wrong, Custis," she said. "There's nothing funny going on here."

For a moment he considered revealing to her that he was a federal lawman. If she knew that, she might be more inclined to tell him the truth.

But he still wanted to keep that card close to his vest right now. At least he would have if he'd been *wearing* a vest, or anything else except his boots, for that matter.

"Listen," he said with genuine concern in his voice. "I ain't lookin' for trouble. If somethin's causin' problems for you and the other folks in Panamint, I'd be glad to do whatever I can to help out. But you got to tell me what it is."

"Nothing!" she cried. "Nothing. Everything . . . everything is . . . fine!"

Except that it obviously wasn't, because she started crying again.

This had sure as hell put a damper on the good mood he'd been in as soon as he got through climaxing inside her, thought Longarm. Other than the fact that both of them were still mostly naked, it was almost like they hadn't even fooled around.

"Blast it, Dallas—" he began.

"Stop it!" She glared up at him. She still looked upset, but she was mad now as well. "Quit harassing me. You need to get out of here right now, Custis. This is still my place, and what I say goes."

He didn't figure she was anywhere near big enough to throw him out, but it wouldn't be very gentlemanly to point that out.

Instead, he straightened and gave her a grim nod. "If that's the way you want it."

"It is." She sniffled. "I . . . I really enjoyed what we did, Custis, but it's over now. You should go."

"What about gettin' together again?"

She shook her head. "That's probably not going to happen. There won't be—"

There won't be what? he asked himself when she broke off in mid-sentence. Won't be a chance? Won't be enough time?

She was acting like the world was about to come to an end. That thought sent another icy shiver dancing along the big lawman's spine.

He reached for his trousers. "I'm gettin' out," he told her, "but this ain't over. I'm gonna find out what's goin' on here in Panamint, and if you folks need my help, you'll get it whether you want it or not."

As he pulled on his clothes, he briefly considered the possibility that Gideon Horne had ridden in and somehow buffaloed the whole town into protecting him. He could have told the citizens that an enemy was on his trail and ordered them to turn Longarm away.

But how in blazes would he get them to go along with that? He'd have to have some sort of mighty powerful hold over them, and for the life of him, Longarm couldn't figure out what that might be.

Unless Horne had taken some hostages, Longarm suddenly thought.

That might make sense. If Horne had gotten his hands on some people that everybody in town cared about . . . some kids, maybe . . . that might give him enough of a bargaining chip to let him bend the townspeople to his will.

If that turned out to be the case, the only way Longarm could stop the outlaw would be to find him and set those hostages loose. Then he would be free to deal with Horne however he saw fit, and the townspeople wouldn't have any reason to stop him.

The more Longarm turned the idea over in his head, the more he was convinced that he had hit upon the truth.

But he didn't let that show on his face. Instead, he buckled on his gun belt and said with a bitter edge in his voice, "I was plannin' to stay here in Panamint for a spell, but I think now that maybe I would be better off takin' my money over to Ballarat. You folks here just lost out, Dallas."

She gave a humorless laugh that held a lot more bitterness than his words. "You're right about that," she said. "We lost out."

Longarm put his hat on and turned to leave. As soon as he was out of earshot of Panamint, he could circle back around and sneak into the settlement, he thought. Then he'd have a look around and see if he could figure out where those hostages were being held.

Assuming that there *were* hostages, of course.

If there weren't, he didn't have any earthly idea what was going on.

"Custis."

He stopped at the doorway and looked back at her, thinking that maybe she had changed her mind about telling him what was wrong.

"Thank you for a good memory," was all she said in a half-whisper.

"It was pretty good, wasn't it?"

He had to give her that much.

The front doors of the Copper Queen were locked, but Dallas had left the key in the lock. Longarm let himself out. He couldn't lock the doors behind him, but he assumed Dallas would come downstairs and take care of that once she had composed herself.

As he paused on the boardwalk in front of the saloon, he looked up and down the long main street. Panamint was laid out in a narrow fashion because it was located in a valley, with ridges looming on either side of it.

Longarm frowned as he looked up at the mountains to the west. It didn't rain often in these parts—Death Valley was one of the driest places on the face of the earth, after all—but when a storm did develop, sometimes it was a real gully washer.

If that happened at just the right place in the mountains and enough water got dumped down, the ridges would funnel it right through town. Panamint would be in danger of being washed away by a flash flood.

The people who had founded the town probably hadn't even thought about that. They had been more concerned with the valuable minerals to be found around here.

Not many lights were burning anymore. Most of the town had rolled up the sidewalks and gone to bed. Longarm didn't see a single soul on the street. No riders, no pedestrians.

Actually, if a fella wanted to be morbid about it, he thought, Panamint didn't just look like it was asleep.

It almost looked dead.

A faint glow came from a livery stable up the street, though. One of the big double doors was open a few inches, and yellow light spilled through it.

Longarm's horse was still tied at one of the hitch rails in front of the Copper Queen. He would need a place to put the animal for the night, and whoever was working at the livery stable might be able to recommend a hotel to him as well.

He went down the three steps to the street, unfastened the reins, and led the horse toward the stable.

If Gideon Horne was here in Panamint, there was a good chance his horse would be at the stable, too. Maybe the hostler could be persuaded to answer a few questions, Longarm thought.

When he reached the stable, he pulled the door open farther and took the horse inside. A lantern with its wick turned low hung on a nail driven into one of the thick beams that supported the ceiling joists.

A broad aisle of hard-packed dirt ran between rows of stalls toward the rear of the barn. Another set of double doors back there probably led out into a corral. To Longarm's left as he came in was a walled-off area that likely served as an office and maybe even the proprietor's living quarters.

The door into that part of the barn was closed. No light shone through the crack underneath it.

"Hello?" Longarm called. "Anybody here?"

There was no answer, so he lifted the reins and led the horse along the aisle until he came to an empty stall. He put the horse in it, stripped saddle and blanket from the animal, and set them on a sawhorse just outside the gate that closed off the stall.

He found a rag and gave the horse a good rubdown. The water trough inside the stall already had water in it. Longarm had spotted a grain bin when he came into the stable. He went to it, filled the bucket that he found in the bin, and brought the grain back to the stall, where he dumped it in an empty feed trough.

"You ought to be all set, old son," he told the horse. "Considerin' all the hell you put me through for a while by runnin' off, I'd say you're gettin' better treatment than you deserve."

The horse ignored him, of course, and started munching on the grain.

Longarm turned away, chuckling and shaking his head. He figured the stablekeeper had gone home for the night, but he could come by here in the morning and settle up with the man when he collected his mount. Such an arrangement wasn't unusual in frontier towns.

But when he stepped out of the stall, he saw something that *was* unusual.

While he was tending to the horse, six men had come into the livery barn. They stood just inside the double doors, blocking Longarm's exit.

He recognized one of them as the shotgun-wielding Tim, who had accosted him as soon as he rode into town. The others were unknown to him, but they had the same sort of raw-boned, dangerous look about them.

"You should'a taken Miss Amelia's advice, mister," Tim said. "Should'a turned your horse around and rode out." He lifted the shotgun. He appeared to be the only one of the five men who was armed. "Unbuckle that gun belt."

Longarm thought about it. The men were far enough away from him that the buckshot would have room to spread out some. It would be hard to avoid those deadly pellets if Tim pulled the Greener's triggers.

The bucket handle was in Longarm's right hand. He'd have to drop it, then reach for his Colt if he wanted to draw the gun. Most men wouldn't even consider trying to outdraw a cocked and leveled shotgun.

Longarm wasn't most men, though, and he didn't like the idea of hollering calf rope. Giving up rubbed him the wrong way.

Still, a man would be a damned fool to argue with a shotgun.

"Take it easy," he told Tim. "You've got the drop on me, old son. I'll put this bucket down, and we can talk."

"Ain't nothin' to talk about," Tim snapped. "I want that gun belt on the ground . . . *now!*"

Slowly, Longarm bent over and set the bucket on the ground. Then he unbuckled the cross-draw rig and took it off. He coiled the belt and placed it and the holstered .44 next to the bucket.

"Step away from it," Tim ordered.

The men with him grinned and began to curl their hands into fists.

"You hombres are makin' a mighty big mistake," warned Longarm. "You don't know—"

"We know enough," Tim cut in. "We know you're gonna wish you'd stayed outta Panamint, mister."

It was time for a gamble, Longarm decided. He said, "Listen, whatever mischief Horne's gotten up to, if we work together we can stop him."

Tim's eyes widened in surprise. "He knows about Horne! Get him!"

Well, that was one bet that hadn't paid off, thought Longarm as the five men with Tim charged him, obviously intent on beating him half to death.

Or maybe even all the way.

Chapter 8

Realizing that Tim had made a mistake by letting the other men get between Longarm and the shotgun, the big lawman made a dive for his gun.

Before he could reach the Colt, one of the men tackled him and drove him off his feet. Longarm flailed toward the revolver but grabbed the handle of the bucket instead.

Facing four to one odds, any weapon was better than none, he supposed.

Longarm swung the bucket, smacking it hard into the head of the man wrestling with him.

That blow knocked the man loose from him and allowed Longarm to roll away. He came up swinging the bucket as the other three tried to close in around him. They jerked back to avoid it.

"Get him, damn it!" Tim yelled again. "He busted Grover's head open!"

Longarm hoped that wasn't true. He wasn't trying to kill anybody. He only wanted to defend himself.

He didn't think these men were actually evil either. They were just desperate for some reason. As they surrounded him, he warned, "You boys back off! I don't want to hurt anybody!"

They hesitated, unwilling to charge him again while he had the bucket in his hand.

"All right, I reckon it's gone too far for that," Tim said. "Get out of the way, fellas."

One of the men glanced at him. "Tim, what the hell are you gonna do?"

Tim swallowed hard. "Only thing I can do. I'm gonna kill this man."

"Damn it, Tim! Nobody said anything about killin'—"

"We got to! You know we can't risk anybody comin' into town and then gettin' back out."

Longarm's heart hammered in his chest. He couldn't get to his Colt now. The men around him blocked him off from it. And his derringer was stowed away in his saddlebags, so it was no good to him either.

But maybe he could make Tim listen to reason. The other men were already leery of the idea of murder. Longarm could see that on their faces.

"You don't want to pull those triggers, Tim," he said. "If you do, you'll be killin' a deputy United States marshal."

That revelation caused Tim's jaw to sag. The other four men looked equally surprised.

"You ain't a marshal," Tim said after a couple of stunned seconds. "You're just a saddle tramp. You told Miss Amelia you was just passin' through."

"That was because I didn't want to reveal who I was just yet. My real name's Custis Long. I'm a deputy U.S. marshal workin' out of the Denver office. For the past two weeks I've been trailin' an outlaw called Gideon Horne. He bushwhacked me a couple of nights ago, and my horse ran off. That gave him a big lead on me before I could catch my horse, but I think he came here to

Panamint." Longarm paused. "I think he's still here, and if you fellas help me catch him, you'll be doin' the right thing. Not only that, but the government'll be grateful to you."

One of the men said, "Tim, maybe he's tellin' the truth. It sure sounds like it."

"Maybe we ought to let him go," another one chimed in.

Longarm saw Tim's determination wavering. The man was the sort of hombre who needed somebody to tell him what to do.

But then his backbone stiffened, literally and figuratively, and he snapped, "You know what Mayor McQuiddy said. Nobody leaves town. Maybe this fella's tellin' the truth about bein' a lawman, and maybe he ain't. But it don't matter either way. We got to lock him up and make sure he don't go nowhere."

"That's almost the same thing as killin' him, ain't it?" one of the men asked with a grim expression on his face.

Tim didn't answer. Instead, he ordered, "Take him down and hog-tie him!"

One of the men shook his head sadly, reached over, and picked up a pitchfork that was leaning against the wall of a stall. "Sorry about this, mister," he said to Longarm, "but you're gonna have to come with us."

Longarm wasn't going to let anybody hog-tie him and lock him up somewhere. Whatever was wrong in Panamint—and it had to be pretty bad, the way everybody in town was acting—he couldn't do anything to help the situation if he was a prisoner.

So as the man approached him, brandishing the pitchfork, Longarm suddenly flipped the bucket around so that he was holding the bottom of it.

Then he rushed straight at the man with the pitchfork. Taken by surprise, the man jerked the fork up and jabbed the tines at Longarm. The mouth of the bucket was wide enough to go over them. The tines struck harmlessly inside the wooden bucket.

Longarm continued to bull forward, and that forced the pitchfork handle back hard into the man's belly. He grunted and turned pale as he doubled over in pain from the unexpected blow.

Longarm threw the bucket and pitchfork aside so that they landed under the feet of another man. That man's legs tangled up with the pitchfork handle, and he fell sprawling on the hard-packed dirt.

Continuing the same move, Longarm pivoted and whipped a roundhouse punch to the jaw of another man. The blow landed with the clean smack of an ax biting into firewood and drove the man sideways. He fell to his knees, stunned.

Longarm grabbed the shirtfront of the fourth man and swung the startled hombre around so that he was between Longarm and Tim's shotgun. The man yelled in alarm as Longarm shoved him straight back into Tim.

Both of them went down. The scattergun flew out of Tim's hands. Luckily, it didn't discharge when it hit the ground.

For a moment, Longarm was the only man left on his feet. He took advantage of that, clubbing his hands together and bringing them down on the back of the neck of the man who had tripped over the pitchfork. The man had been trying to get up, but the wallop sent him back to the ground, out cold this time.

The man who'd been poked in the belly by the pitchfork handle lay curled on his side, wheezing as he tried to catch his breath. Longarm didn't think he would be much of a threat for a while.

The other four were still down, although Tim had

managed to get to his hands and knees and was scrambling to retrieve his shotgun.

Longarm scooped up his Colt and fired, putting the .44 slug into the dirt between Tim and the Greener. Tim stopped so short that he took a nosedive into the ground.

Circling around the men, Longarm covered them until he reached the shotgun. He bent down and picked up the double-barreled weapon.

"I've had enough of this waltzin' around," he said angrily. "I don't know what's goin' on in this town, but you damn fools won't make it any better by attackin' a lawman."

Tim looked up at him. "Are you really a federal marshal?"

"Dammit, I'm a deputy U.S. marshal like I told you. I'd show you my badge and bona fides, but I ain't in much of a mood to do it." Longarm stepped back, tucked the Colt behind his belt since the cross-draw rig was still lying on the ground, and covered the men with the shotgun instead. "All of you get on your feet. Help those fellas who're sort of groggy."

He was referring to the man who'd been clubbed to the ground and knocked out momentarily and the one Longarm had clouted with the bucket, whose head wasn't busted open after all. Both men were starting to come to now.

Within a couple of minutes, all six men were standing and partly alert again. Longarm kept an eye on them and watched the doors of the livery barn at the same time.

People could have heard that shot he'd fired. For all he knew, more of Panamint's citizens were lurking outside, waiting to ambush him if he came out of the barn.

So he motioned with the shotgun's twin barrels and said, "You fellas are goin' out first. Get movin'."

Stubbornly, they didn't budge. "Where are we goin'?" Tim demanded.

"You're gonna take me to Gideon Horne," Longarm said.

Tim blanched, and so did the other men. Tim began, "I don't know what you're—"

Longarm silenced him by lifting the shotgun's barrels a little. "Don't lie to me," the big lawman said. "Horne's here in Panamint, and we all know it. So you can either take me to him, or start tellin' me everything you know about what's going on around here."

Tim and the other men exchanged glances. One of them said, "He already knows about Horne, Tim."

"Yeah, and he's a lawman," another man put in. "I don't want to get in bad with the law."

A harsh laugh came from Tim. "You think gettin' in trouble with the law really matters now, Rulon? You think that?"

The man flushed. "There ain' nothin' sayin' that we're *all* gonna die. Some of us might make it, and if I'm one of 'em, I don't want to be locked up."

This was getting more and more loco, thought Longarm. It seemed like everybody in Panamint was worried that they were in imminent danger of dying for some reason. That explained the fatalistic attitude Tim displayed, and Dallas Farrar, too.

But it didn't explain why they felt that way.

Figuring that out could wait. Right now, Longarm wanted to know where Gideon Horne was.

"I've had a bad couple of days, Tim," he said. "I'm through arguin' with you. Take me to Horne, or you'll be damned sorry."

"I'm already damn sorry, mister," Tim said. He heaved a sigh. "But I reckon takin' you to Horne ain't gonna make anything worse than it already is."

Longarm nodded. "Now you're thinkin' straight." He jerked the Greener's barrels toward the barn doors. "Let's go."

The men marched out of the barn, and Longarm followed them, keeping the shotgun trained on them. On the way out, he scooped up his gun belt and draped it over his shoulder.

He hoped that by sending the men out first, he would defuse any trap that the other townspeople might have laid for him. Nothing happened, though.

It appeared that the gunshot in the barn hadn't drawn any attention, as unlikely as that seemed.

Either that, or everybody in Panamint was just too afraid to come out tonight.

Icy fingers played up and down Longarm's spine again, but he did his best to ignore them as Tim and the other men turned toward the end of town where Dr. Amelia Judd's house was located.

A frown creased Longarm's forehead. Maybe Horne was hurt. It was certainly possible that one of the shots Longarm had fired at him the night before had wounded him.

But if that was the case, why were the townspeople so scared?

"Where are we goin', Tim?" Longarm called softly.

"You'll see when we get there, damn it. I'm takin' you to Horne, like you said for me to do."

Longarm spotted the house that he assumed belonged to Dr. Judd. As they approached it, one of the men said nervously, "You don't need us to come with you, Marshal. Tim knows where he's goin'."

"If I let you go, what's to stop you from tryin' to jump me again?" Longarm asked.

"That scattergun, for one thing. For another . . ." The man dragged the back of his hand across his mouth.

"For another thing, I'm done with this. I just want to go back home to my wife and kids. I'm sorry we tried to hurt you, Marshal."

"Me, too," added one of the other men. "We just didn't know what to do."

Muttered agreement came from the other men.

They all sounded so frightened and miserable that Longarm found himself believing them. They were too scared to be lying. He said, "Hold up a minute," and they all halted.

Longarm thought it over for a moment and shrugged. "All right, get the hell out of here," he told them. "All except you, Tim."

"Yeah, I figured that," Tim said with a note of bitter irony in his voice.

"Sorry, Tim," one of the men said. Then he and the others scurried off into the night, heading for their homes.

"Let's go," Longarm said, and once again he and Tim resumed their walk down the street.

As Longarm expected, Tim turned in at the gate in the fence around the house's small front yard. Longarm followed closely behind him.

They were halfway up the flagstone walk to the porch when the house's front door opened and a man's voice asked, "Who's there? I have a gun. I'll shoot if I have to!" The words had a nervous quaver to them.

"It's me, Mayor," Tim said.

"Who's that with you? Did you . . . take care of that matter?"

Longarm stepped a little to the side so that the man on the porch could see him better, including the shotgun.

"If you mean, did they beat me up and run me out of town, nope, they sure didn't," he said. The words caused the figure on the porch to stiffen in surprise and possibly fear. "If you've really got a gun, Mayor, I'd advise you not to use it. Even if you got lead in me, it wouldn't stop me from pullin' the triggers on this Greener, and anyway, I'm a dadgum deputy U.S. marshal."

"A . . . a marshal!" the man on the porch gasped. "You came here . . . after Horne?"

"That's right," Longarm said.

The mayor laughed, but it wasn't a pretty sound. "You're too late. He's dying!"

"What in blazes are you talkin' about?"

Another figure appeared on the porch, stepping out through the dimly lit doorway. Longarm knew from the silhouette that this newcomer was a woman, so he wasn't surprised to hear Dr. Judd's voice.

"Did I hear correctly?" she asked. "You're a federal marshal?"

"That's right, ma'am," Longarm told her.

She sighed. "You might as well come on in, Marshal. It's too late to try to hide things from you now."

"Darned right it is," Longarm agreed. He prodded Tim with the shotgun's barrels. "Get on in there."

Tim hesitated. "I don't want to," he said over his shoulder. "I don't much care if you shoot me."

Dr. Judd said, "You don't have to be like that, Tim. I hate to say it, but you've already been exposed. Half the town probably has been. You can come in."

"Exposed?" Longarm repeated. "Are you sayin'—"

"That's right, Marshal." The doctor moved to the top of the porch steps. "Gideon Horne is dying of cholera, and it's highly likely that before this is over, a great many others here in Panamint will be, too."

Chapter 9

Cholera!

Like wildfire, which it resembled in the speed with which it could spread, the disease was greatly feared. Longarm had read in the newspapers about great outbreaks of it that had spread across Asia and Europe, killing tens or even hundreds of thousands.

Cholera epidemics had struck in the United States, too. The malady had laid low many people back in the crowded cities of the East, as well as in the gold fields of California during the Gold Rush days.

It struck from time to time even in frontier settlements, wiping out half a town in a matter of days like the grim horseman of Death had ridden through, swinging his scythe.

If they had cholera here in Panamint, Longarm could understand why everybody was so afraid.

"You're sure that's what it is?" he asked.

"Positive," Dr. Judd said. "All the symptoms are correct. The sudden weakness, the terrible evacuations of the bowels, the resulting dehydration of the patient . . .

It's cholera, all right, Marshal. Do you have any medical training?"

Longarm shook his head. "Just how to patch up bullet wounds and broken legs and such, the sort of things that I've learned from experience."

"Then I wouldn't question my diagnosis if I were you."

"I'm not questionin' anything, ma'am... I mean, Doctor. If you say it's cholera, I believe you. You say a lot of folks in town have already been exposed to it?"

"That's right." Dr. Judd sighed. "You might as well come in. You won't be in any more danger by doing that than you already are. And for goodness' sake, stop waving that shotgun around. It might go off accidentally and hurt someone."

Longarm didn't bother telling her that no gun had ever gone off accidentally in his hands. Not when he was a boy in West-by God-Virginia, and not since then either.

Instead, he just lowered the Greener's barrels until they were pointing toward the ground.

In a surly voice, Tim said, "You don't need me anymore, I reckon."

"No, that's all right, go on," Longarm told him.

"Wait a minute, Tim," the doctor said sharply. "I'd like to know why you brought the marshal here."

Tim shuffled his feet and rolled his shoulders in embarrassment. "I know how you and the mayor said it was so important that nobody find out about us havin' that sickness here, so since this hombre wouldn't leave town, some of the boys and me decided to rough him up a mite and, uh, persuade him to light a shuck. He whipped us, though," Tim added bitterly.

"Tim, Tim." Dr. Judd shook her head sadly. "That wouldn't have done any good. Once the marshal spent time here, he was exposed, too."

Tim rubbed his jaw and said, "Yeah, I reckon we didn't think about that."

"It's more important now that no one leave town. We don't want to spread the disease to other settlements." Her voice firmed with determination. "We must contain the outbreak *here*. It's possible that it may not become an epidemic. It's not even outside the realm of possibility that Mr. Horne may not die. People have been known to recover from a bout of cholera."

The mayor turned to her, hope springing into his voice as he asked, "Really? You mean, it might not wipe out the town? I was hoping, but I didn't know . . ."

"We can only hope for the best," the doctor said. "Come in, Marshal . . . is your name really Parker?"

"No, ma'am," Longarm told her. "It's Long, Custis Long."

"Then come in, Marshal Long, and we can tell you what's happened here in the past twenty-four hours."

Longarm broke the shotgun open, pulled the shells from the barrels, snapped the weapon closed, and handed it to Tim. He dropped the shells into the man's other hand.

"Just so you know, I don't much cotton to havin' guns pointed at me," he said. "It might not work out so good for you if you ever try it again."

"Don't you worry, Marshal. I plan on steerin' clear of you as much as I can."

Longarm nodded. "Good idea."

He took the Colt from behind his belt, slid it into its holster, and strapped the gun belt around his hips. He went up the steps to the porch and joined Dr. Judd and the mayor.

"Marshal Long, this is A.P. McQuiddy, the mayor of Panamint," the doctor said.

Longarm nodded to the man but didn't offer to shake hands. "Mayor."

McQuiddy took a handkerchief from his coat pocket and mopped nervously at his face. "Marshal," he said. "Under normal circumstances, I'd be glad to meet you, especially with a notorious outlaw like Gideon Horne in our community. I'm afraid these circumstances are anything but normal, though."

Dr. Judd led them into the house. The front room was set up as an office and examining room. Several doors opened off a hallway that ran toward the rear of the house. The doctor's living quarters were probably back there.

"Mr. Horne is in the first room," Dr. Judd said. She went to the open door and indicated that Longarm should precede her.

He tried not to hesitate as he stepped into the doorway, but he couldn't keep his skin from crawling a little. The sour, rotten smell of sickness filled the room. The curtains were closed over the window, which kept out fresh air and made the smell worse.

A lamp with the wick turned down low sat on a small table next to a narrow bed and cast a dim light over the man who lay there. Longarm didn't know if it was the bad light or the illness that gripped Gideon Horne, but the outlaw didn't look good at all. He was a far cry from dashing and handsome now.

The dark hair with its white stripe was tangled and damp with sweat. Horne's face was gaunt and washed out. His eyes seemed to have sunk into his head. They were closed, and for a second Longarm thought he was dead.

But the sheet pulled up over Horne's chest was rising and falling slightly, Longarm saw. Horne was still alive . . . for now.

"What happened?" asked Longarm. "Was he like this when he got here?"

McQuiddy shook his head. "No, he seemed fine. I've talked to folks who saw him ride in and spoke to him. He went straight to the Copper Queen and had some drinks there. He ate supper at Donnelly's Café and got a room at the Panamint House and put his horse up at the livery stable. The same sort of things that any fella would do when he rode into a town he was just passing through."

Longarm nodded. "So he moved around a lot in the settlement, did he?"

"That's right," Dr. Judd said. "Spreading infection everywhere he went."

"But he didn't seem to be sick at the time," McQuiddy pointed out. "Nobody knew anything was wrong with him until one of the maids at the hotel found him this morning, passed out next to his bed, as if he'd tried to get up and couldn't make it." The mayor's nose wrinkled. "The bed linens were, ah, quite fouled. It appeared as if he'd had too much to drink."

"Joel Guthrie, the owner of the hotel, had several men carry him down here to my place. He was coming around a bit at that point and seemed like perhaps he might be okay," Dr. Judd resumed the story again. "But I knew immediately that it wasn't alcohol that was the problem." She sighed. "I made the mistake of mentioning the word *cholera* where one of the men could hear it . . ."

"And that was all it took," guessed Longarm.

She nodded. "Yes. The news was spreading all over town in a matter of minutes." She looked at McQuiddy. "I'll give the mayor credit. He called a town meeting right away and calmed everyone down, told them what they needed to do."

Longarm turned his gaze to McQuiddy. "Which was what?"

"Why, keep their wits about them, of course," said McQuiddy. "Panic wasn't going to do any good. The contagion was already loose in our town. There was nothing we could do to stop it. But we *could* contain it."

"By not letting anybody in or out of town."

McQuiddy nodded. "That's right. My hope was that perhaps the sickness would run its course and then be over and done with. Panamint might survive. But if anybody knew we'd had the cholera here, no one would ever come here again. They'd go to one of the other towns around here . . ."

"And Panamint would wither and die," said Longarm.

With a sigh, the mayor nodded again. "That's right."

Dr. Judd said, "Mayor McQuiddy was actually doing the right thing by quarantining the town, although his motives were economic rather than medical. By keeping everyone who's been exposed to the disease isolated, we can stop it from spreading. In a week or two, who knows, this may all be over."

"That's what I'm praying for," McQuiddy said fervently.

"All right, I reckon I understand," Longarm said. "Horne's too sick to be moved, and I wouldn't want to anyway, since that might spread the sickness. What are the warnin' signs when an hombre's about to come down with it, Doc?"

A sudden smile flashed across Amelia Judd's face. Longarm's attention had been focused on Gideon Horne, so he hadn't really noticed until then how pretty the doctor was. She was about thirty, he judged, with masses of midnight dark hair piled on her head and a nice shape under the white blouse and long skirt.

"What?" he asked her.

"I don't believe anyone's ever called me 'Doc' before," she said. "I have enough trouble just convincing people that I actually am both a woman and a doctor."

"Well, the woman part of it is pretty evident."

She smiled again before growing serious. "To answer your question, Marshal, there aren't really any warning signs. A slight listlessness, perhaps. But the primary symptoms come on quickly. The first evacuation often takes people by surprise."

Yeah, nobody really expected to start shitting themselves to death, thought Longarm. That was what cholera did. It took away every bit of a man's dignity, all the moisture in his body, and finally his life.

"There's really not much I can do for someone stricken with the disease either," Dr. Judd went on. "I'm just trying to keep Mr. Horne as comfortable as possible and replace as much of the fluid in his body as I can get down him. It's a difficult battle, though."

"One that the sawbones usually don't win," Longarm commented.

She nodded again. "I'm afraid so. The odds are high against Mr. Horne recovering."

Longarm looked over at the mayor. "Has anybody else in town come down with this stuff?"

"Not yet," McQuiddy replied with a shake of his head. "Not that I know of anyway. But I'm sure it's just a matter of time." He gazed down at the man in the bed, and anger burned in his eyes. "I know I shouldn't say it, but damn that man for bringing this pestilence to our town!"

"Did Horne tell folks who he was when he rode in?"

"He told people his name. No one really realized at the time that he was a fugitive, though. What did he do?"

"Robbed a train down in Texas and killed a deputy

U.S. marshal in El Paso. Friend of mine named Bert Collins."

"I'm sorry, Marshal. If we had known . . ." McQuiddy's voice drifted off, and he shook his head. "Well, to be honest, even if we had known, there wouldn't be much we could do about it. We have a constable here in Panamint who breaks up fights in the saloons and things like that, but no real law enforcement. I'm not sure anyone would have been willing to try to capture an actual outlaw."

"Not your job," Longarm agreed. "But I've caught up to him now, and if he makes it, I'll take him back to face justice for what he's done." The big lawman shrugged. "If the cholera takes him . . . well, I reckon it saves the price of a hang rope."

"You're forgetting something, Marshal," Dr. Judd said. "You've been exposed to the disease, too. You may not survive to take him in."

"If I don't, that's the way the hand plays out," Longarm said with the sort of grim, fatalistic acceptance that developed in any man whose job involved risking his life on a daily basis. It was like a callus on his soul, something always there that he seldom thought about.

Longarm was curious about something else. He nodded toward Horne and asked, "Where do you reckon he picked it up?"

"The cholera? There's no way of knowing. Somewhere back down the trail, I suppose."

Longarm gave his earlobe a couple of tugs. Dr. Judd was right. They would probably never know the answer to that question.

Mayor McQuiddy said, "I'm sorry you're having to deal with such a terrible business so soon after you came here, Doctor."

Longarm glanced at the doctor. "You haven't been in Panamint long, Doc?"

She shook her head. "Just about a month."

"First doctor we've had in a while," McQuiddy said with a note of pride in his voice. "There was an old drunk who patched people up, but he passed on. A town can't call itself a real town without a real doctor."

"You're probably right about that," Longarm said.

Horne let out a little moan and shifted slightly in the bed.

Dr. Judd waved Longarm and McQuiddy toward the door. "The two of you go on now. I'll tend to him."

"I can stay and help," Longarm offered.

She shook her head. "I don't mean to be rude, Marshal, but I don't need any help. I can do everything that needs to be done. I may be a woman, but I'm not exactly what you'd call a delicate flower."

"I can see that," Longarm said.

Chapter 10

Longarm and McQuiddy left the doctor's house, stepping out into the quiet black night.

"What are your plans now, Marshal?" the mayor asked.

"Like I said inside, I'll have to wait and see whether Horne lives or dies."

McQuiddy shook his head. "No, I was talking about your immediate plans."

"I suppose I'll get a room in the hotel. But *not* the room Horne was stayin' in," Longarm added. "No sense in uppin' the odds of catchin' that unholy stuff."

A shudder went through the mayor. "I should say not. I believe Joel Guthrie has that particular room locked and won't let anybody in there."

"Wise move."

"I'll come with you to the hotel and make sure Joel knows who you are, so you'll be treated properly."

Longarm shook his head. "I don't mind the company, Mayor, but I don't need any special treatment."

"I wouldn't say that. The town is lucky that you came along when you did, Marshal Long. I've been able to maintain order, but it hasn't been easy. When the news spread about the cholera, a lot of people wanted to leave town. I had a difficult job convincing them they'd be better off staying. Dr. Judd helped me make them understand that they've already been exposed, so all they'd be doing by leaving would be spreading the disease."

"I'd say Panamint's a lot luckier to have the doc around than me."

"She's been a rock, that's for sure," McQuiddy agreed with a fervent nod.

"Where'd she come from?" Longarm asked as the two men walked up the street toward the hotel.

"Before she moved here, you mean?" McQuiddy shook his head. "I don't really know. I can't recall her ever talking about her past. Why do you ask, Marshal?"

"Oh, just curious," replied Longarm. "It ain't often you run into a lady doc, especially one that pretty. Especially— and I don't mean no offense by this, Mayor—in a rough mining town on the edge of Death Valley."

McQuiddy rubbed his chin. "You know, I never really thought about it like that, Marshal. You're right. I'll bet there's a story behind why Dr. Judd is here. But we may never know it. She's a very private person."

"That's her right, I reckon." Longarm stopped and nodded toward the two-story frame building they had reached. "This is the hotel, eh?"

"There are a couple of others in Panamint, but this is the best one," McQuiddy said. He ushered Longarm inside.

Joel Guthrie, the proprietor of the Panamint House, turned out to be a tall, slender gent with iron gray hair and the same sort of worried expression that everybody else in the settlement wore right now. He had his elbows on the desk in the lobby, but he straightened as Longarm and McQuiddy came in.

"A.P.," he greeted the mayor. "Is there any news?"

McQuiddy shook his head. "Nope. That fella Horne is still alive, or at least he was when Marshal Long and I left the doctor's house a few minutes ago."

Guthrie frowned as he looked at Longarm and repeated, "Marshal?"

McQuiddy grunted. "I'm surprised you haven't heard the news already. This is Deputy U.S. Marshal Long. Turns out Gideon Horne is a wanted outlaw. Marshal Long's been trailing him."

Guthrie said, "I wish to God you'd caught him and killed him before the bastard ever made it to Panamint, Marshal."

"Can't say as I blame you," Longarm said.

"The marshal needs a room," McQuiddy put in. "He's going to stay here in town and wait to see if Horne recovers."

"Don't you mean wait to see if we all die?"

Longarm shrugged. "I suppose it might come to that. But there's nothin' we can do except wait, is there?"

Guthrie shook his head and sighed. "No, there's not." A hollow laugh came from him. "There are several vacant rooms in the hotel, Marshal. You can have your pick. No charge, of course."

"I don't mind payin'."

"No need. It's not like you're keeping a paying customer from taking the room."

"Well, that's true," Longarm admitted. "Got anything overlookin' the street?"

"As a matter of fact, I do." Guthrie turned and took a key from the rack on the wall behind him. "Room Eleven. Straight ahead on your right at the top of the stairs. Do you have any bags?"

Longarm picked up the key Guthrie slid across the desk to him and shook his head. "I left all my gear over at the livery stable with my horse."

"That's fine. You can't worry about a man running out on the bill when he's not paying for the room, can you?" Guthrie laughed humorlessly again. "And even if he did, that'd be the least of your worries in a case like this, wouldn't it?"

Longarm didn't know what to say to that comment. Everybody in Panamint was acting like they were half-way up the thirteen steps to the gallows.

He couldn't really blame them for feeling that way. Cholera was a terrible thing.

"I'll see you in the morning, Marshal," McQuiddy said. "If you'd like, come over to Donnelly's and join me for breakfast." The mayor smiled solemnly. "As long as we're healthy, we need to keep our strength up. We'll need it if we get sick."

"Sure, Mayor." Longarm lifted a hand in farewell. "See you in the mornin'."

"We can all hope," McQuiddy muttered under his breath as he turned away.

Longarm said good night to Guthrie and went up the stairs. He found Room Eleven. The door was unlocked.

It was a typical frontier hotel room, Longarm saw as he snapped a lucifer to life with his thumbnail and lit the lamp on the bedside table. Nothing fancy about it. A bed, a couple of chairs, a table, a dresser. Thin curtains over the single window and a little rug on the floor next to the bed.

Longarm pushed the curtains aside for a moment and raised the window, feeling the need to get some fresh air into the room. He fished a cheroot out of his shirt pocket and lit another match to set fire to the gasper.

He hung his hat on one of the posts at the foot of the bed and sat down in a ladderback chair to take his boots off. Smoke wreathed his head as he puffed on the cheroot.

The mundane task of removing his boots left his mind free to wander. A lot had happened since he rode in, and his thoughts raced back over everything he had seen and heard following his arrival in Panamint.

He was sure of one thing now: Dallas Farrar had acted so brazenly and gotten him into her bed right away because she really *was* afraid that she'd never have the opportunity to be with a man again. Gideon Horne had spent some time in the Copper Queen, so according to Dr. Amelia Judd, he might have infected everybody in the saloon.

The thought that Dallas had bedded him so eagerly because he was handy made a wry smile come to Longarm's lips.

That hadn't been all of it, he told himself. There were other men in the place she could have gone after. She had wanted him, and despite the fact that Longarm didn't really have an ounce of vanity in his body, he was glad he had been more than a matter of convenience to the beautiful redhead.

He put his gun belt on the chair next to the bed and stripped down to the bottom half of his long johns. He finished the cheroot and blew out the lamp before climbing into bed.

After the past couple of rough days, he might have expected to doze off quickly.

Sleep didn't come, though. Instead, he found himself staring up at the darkened ceiling. The feeling that something was wrong scurried around in the back of his mind like a crazed weasel nipping at his brain.

At least one person had lied to him tonight. That was his hunch, and he had learned to trust his hunches. They had kept him alive more than once.

His stomach rumbled, followed immediately by a clench of cold fear. Was he getting sick?

Then he realized that with everything that had happened, he had never gotten around to eating any supper. In fact, he couldn't remember the last time he had eaten.

He grinned in the darkness and told himself, "You're just hungry, old son."

The idea of getting up, getting dressed again, and going out to find something to eat wasn't that appealing, but Longarm knew he wouldn't be able to sleep with his belly empty and growling like a bear that had just gotten up from a long winter's hibernation.

He sat up and swung his legs out of bed.

His feet had just touched the floor when a boot slammed into the door beside the knob and knocked it wide open with a splintering crash.

Muzzle flame lanced through the darkness, like lightning accompanied by the crash of gun thunder.

Instinct took over as bullets whipped past the big lawman's head. Longarm dived off the bed. His hand flashed out unerringly to snag the Colt from its holster.

He hit the floor, rolled, and came up shooting. The .44 roared and bucked in his hand as he triggered two swift shots.

The intruder wasn't done yet. His guns continued to blast away, tracking Longarm's muzzle flashes now.

Longarm flattened out on the floor and tipped the Colt's barrel upward. He pulled the trigger again and sent flame stabbing from the barrel.

The shadowy shape of the intruder reeled and staggered toward the doorway. The man threw two more quick shots at Longarm as he fled.

Rapid footsteps pounded in the hotel corridor outside the room. The gunman was trying to get away.

Longarm surged to his feet, ready to give chase even though he wore only his long underwear. He grabbed the gun belt from the chair. He was liable to need the fresh ammunition he carried in the belt's loops.

His natural caution slowed him as he reached the doorway. It was possible the varmint had stopped down the hall and was waiting for him to stick his head out.

Longarm went out in a low crouch, his gun swiveling in the direction the would-be killer had fled.

The hall was empty, but Longarm caught a glimpse of a moving shadow at its far end, away from the stairs that led up from the lobby. He ran along the corridor, and as he came closer, he saw the top of a narrow staircase at the end of the hall. The hotel probably had a side entrance at the bottom of those stairs.

Again wary of a trap, Longarm poked his head and his gun around the corner of the staircase. He didn't see anything, although the light from the upstairs hall filtered only dimly into the stairwell. He started down, moving quietly as well as quickly.

The stairs turned back on themselves in a tiny landing halfway to the ground floor. As Longarm went around that corner, again crouching low, a gun blasted at the bottom of the stairs. He felt the wind rip of the bullet past his ear.

Longarm's .44 thundered twice. Here in this narrow stairwell, the noise was deafening. Before the echoes from the reports even had a chance to start to fade, he rushed down the stairs.

No more shots greeted him. When he reached the bottom, he found an open door leading out into a dark, narrow alley beside the hotel.

Longarm paused long enough to buckle on the gun belt and thumb fresh cartridges into the chambers of the Colt's cylinder. He didn't leave one of the chambers empty this time, as most men who packed iron were in the habit of doing. Figuring that he might need a full wheel, he loaded all six.

With the Colt in his hand, he stepped out into the darkness and pressed his bare back against the wall of the building.

For a moment, the roar of gunshots had filled his head so that he couldn't hear anything else. That was starting to fade now, and his hearing was coming back.

He grimaced as a swift rataplan of hoofbeats drifted to his ears through the cool night air. That would be the assassin fleeing, he thought. The gunman had probably left his horse tethered here by the side door and crept up those stairs on his deadly errand. That way he wouldn't have had to go through the lobby, where Joel Guthrie or someone else might have seen him.

Longarm waited until the sound of the running horse diminished to nothing. Muttering "son of a bitch" under his breath, he unloaded one of the chambers in the Colt and eased the hammer down on the empty. He was tucking the cartridge back into an empty loop on the shell belt when footsteps sounded inside the hotel.

"Who's out there? I've got a gun, and I'll shoot if I have to!"

Longarm recognized the proprietor's voice. He said, "Take it easy, Mr. Guthrie. It's me, Custis Long."

"Marshal?" Guthrie sounded surprised. "I heard a bunch of shooting. What the hell is going on?"

Longarm didn't holster his Colt just yet. He stepped back into the hotel and saw Guthrie's silhouette against the light that came down a hall from the lobby.

"Somebody kicked open the door of my room and tried to kill me," he said. "I reckon the door's busted and there are probably quite a few bullet holes in the bed. Sorry for the damages."

"Good Lord! You don't have to apologize, Marshal. I'm the one who's sorry that . . . that such a terrible thing could happen in my hotel!"

"Did anybody come in through the lobby in the last fifteen minutes or so?"

Guthrie shook his head. "No. I'll admit, I've been dozing a little, but I think I would have woken up if anyone had come in."

Longarm gestured toward the side door. "You leave this unlocked most of the time?"

"Yes, of course. It's more convenient for some of the guests to come and go that way."

"And people in these parts know that?"

Guthrie shrugged. "I suppose some of them do. It's not like it's a secret or anything." He paused. "Are you all right, Marshal? Were you wounded?"

"Nope, luck was on my side tonight."

"What about the man who tried to kill you? Did you see him? Do you know who he was?"

"No idea," Longarm replied honestly.

"Why would anybody try to do such a thing?"

"I intend to find out," Longarm said.

Chapter 11

Guthrie went back upstairs with Longarm. When Longarm lit the lamp in his room, he carried it over by the doorway and let the light wash over the floor.

"Look there," he said as he pointed to a couple of splashes of crimson on the planks.

"Is that blood?" Guthrie asked in a hollow voice.

"It sure is. Appears that I ventilated the son of a bitch."

Guthrie sniffed the gunsmoke-laden air and looked around in the room in dismay. "You can't stay here, Marshal," he declared. "Let me get you the key to Room Fifteen. It's just down the hall."

Longarm nodded. "Much obliged."

"I'd like to collect for the damages from the man who did this," Guthrie said. "But at least he had to pay a little in blood."

Once Guthrie had brought him the key to the other room, Longarm gathered up his clothes and went down the hall. Room Fifteen was almost a twin to Room Eleven, although the spread on the bed had a different pattern and the curtains over the window were a different color.

Longarm didn't care about any of that. He pulled his clothes on and went downstairs after locking his door.

He wedged a tiny piece of broken matchstick between the door and the jamb. It was a favorite trick of his. If the matchstick was on the floor when he got back, he would know that someone had been in his room . . . and might still be in there.

Wounded or not, whoever wanted him dead might not give up after one try.

Guthrie looked up in surprise behind the desk as Longarm came down the stairs to the lobby. "Something else wrong, Marshal?" he asked.

Longarm shook his head. "Nope. Just before that varmint busted in and started burnin' powder, I realized I didn't have any supper. I was just gettin' up to get dressed when the shootin' started, which probably saved my life. Is there anyplace around here where I can get something to eat this late?"

Longarm knew the hour was after midnight by now.

Guthrie nodded. "Cletus Donnelly keeps his café open all night. The crews at the silver mill work around the clock, so there's always someone who needs something to eat."

Longarm had noticed the continuous rumble from the stamp mill at the far end of town. "Must be a lot of ore, if they're pressin' it into ingots twenty-four hours a day."

"They don't mold it into ingots," Guthrie said with a smile. "When the mines first started up around here, there was a lot of trouble with shipments being held up. So somebody came up with the idea of molding the silver into giant balls."

Longarm frowned. "Giant balls?" he repeated.

"That's right. The sort of thing you'd fire from the biggest cannon that ever existed. They must weigh close to five hundred pounds each."

Longarm thought about it and had to chuckle. "Not exactly something you could stick in your hip pocket and walk off with, is that the idea?"

"It takes a lot of men and equipment to load them up and sturdy wagons to carry them out of here and down to the railroad. As far as I know, the mine owners haven't had any trouble with robberies since they started doing it that way."

Longarm shook his head. When it came to making money, folks would always figure out a way.

He got directions to the café and set out in search of a late supper.

Since somebody had already tried to kill him once tonight, he pushed his normal alertness up a notch and was ready to draw his gun as he made his way along the street.

Nothing happened. Panamint still appeared to be asleep for the most part.

Donnelly's Café was all lit up, however, just like Guthrie had said it would be. Longarm went inside and found it to be a cheery place with at least a dozen tables covered with red-checked tablecloths. Men in rough work clothes were eating at several of the tables. A short, stocky, balding man in a white apron stood behind a counter to the right.

"Evening, mister," he greeted Longarm. "What can I do for you?"

"I could use something to eat. A steak, maybe."

The man nodded. "Sure thing. Supper trimmings, or breakfast? This late at night, I have both ready."

"Make it breakfast," replied Longarm with a grin. Even though he was going to bed from here, having some flapjacks and eggs along with his steak sounded mighty good.

"Coming up," the man said. "Sit anywhere you want. Coffee?"

Longarm nodded. No matter what hour of the night or day, a cup of Arbuckles never bothered his sleep like it seemed to some folks.

Longarm took one of the stools at the counter. The man in the apron poured the coffee for him, then reached under the bar and brought up a bottle.

"Little sweetener?" he asked.

Longarm saw the label proclaiming the contents of the bottle to be Maryland rye. His grin widened.

"You're a kindred spirit, Mr. Donnelly," he said. "You *are* Cletus Donnelly?"

"That's right." Donnelly splashed a little of the liquor into the coffee cup, then extended his hand to shake with the big lawman. "And I'm betting you're that marshal I've heard about."

"Custis Long," Longarm confirmed as he shook with the man.

"I'll get that steak for you."

Donnelly disappeared through a door into the kitchen.

When he came back a few minutes later and set a platter full of steaming hot food on the counter, Longarm commented, "You're one of the few people I've met in Panamint tonight who don't seem scared half out of his wits by the cholera."

Donnelly's brawny shoulders rose and fell in a shrug. "Were you in the war, Marshal?"

"I took part in the Late Unpleasantness," Longarm admitted. "Just don't ask me on which side. That was so long ago I sort of disremember."

Donnelly nodded. "I know exactly what you mean. I was there, too, and one day my company got caught in an artillery barrage when we tried to cross a field. Those shells rained down on us like a thunderstorm, Marshal. There was nothing we could do except keep moving. I had shells burst in front of me, behind me, and on both sides of me. But somehow I made it to the trees on the other side of the field without a scratch on me. Seven of us lived that day. The rest of the company was wiped out. But I was the only one without even a scratch on me."

"Lucky man," said Longarm.

"Yeah. I should've been dead that day. So I figure everything that's come after that . . . well, hell, it's just gravy, isn't it? If my time runs out now, it runs out. Worrying about it won't do a damn bit of good."

"You're a wise man, Mr. Donnelly," Longarm said.

"Thank you, Marshal." Donnelly gestured toward the food. "Now dig in while it's hot."

Longarm did so. The steak was cooked just the way he liked it, the flapjacks and eggs and hash brown potatoes likewise. Washed down with the spiked coffee, the meal was enough to make a man feel downright human again.

A couple of the workers came up to the counter to pay Donnelly for their meals. One of them commented, "Got to get back to work, dang it."

Donnelly smiled at the man. "No rest for the wicked, eh, Frank?"

Frank grunted. "You got that right, boyo. You'd think the bosses might close down the stamp mill for a while, since we got cholera in town, but it don't look like that's gonna happen. We got to keep workin', they say."

"The bosses got big bosses," Donnelly pointed out. "And I don't imagine they care too much about what else is going on in Panamint. They just want that silver to keep flowing."

"Yeah, that's the truth. They'll be up a creek, though, if everybody dies from that damned sickness. Who's gonna work the mines and the mill then?"

Longarm looked over at the man and asked, "Is any-body else sick yet?"

The man frowned. "Not that I know of. Why do you ask, mister?"

"Just wonderin'. Horne turned up sick yesterday mornin', and a lot of people were around him the night before that."

"They'll start droppin' like flies anytime now," the mill worker predicted glumly. He put a grimy hand on his belly. "Every time I feel a little twinge, I think it's the beginnin' of the end for me."

The other men nodded in agreement.

"Maybe it won't turn out that way," said Longarm. "Maybe you'll all be lucky."

"Yeah, maybe I'll sprout wings and pick up one of them damn big silver balls and fly off to the moon with it, too!"

Longarm couldn't argue with that, so he just smiled, shook his head, and went back to his meal. The workers trooped out, heading back to their jobs.

When Longarm was finished, he slid a coin across the counter to Donnelly. "Much obliged," he said. "I might just come back in the mornin' for a second breakfast."

"I'll be here," Donnelly told him.

"When do you sleep?"

"I don't, much. When you come as close as I did to getting blown up, you want to enjoy every moment you've got left."

"I suppose so," Longarm said. He lifted a hand in fare-well and left the café.

He paused outside to light a cheroot, glancing toward the far end of town where the stamp mill kept up its racket as he did so. He shook out the lucifer and tossed it into the street.

Setting fire to the gasper like that had been deliberate.

He was making a target of himself if anybody cared to take a shot at him again. That was one way to lure whoever wanted him dead back out into the open.

Nothing happened. After a moment he started back toward the hotel.

Joel Guthrie must have turned in for the night. The lobby was deserted. Longarm walked through it and went upstairs.

The tiny piece of matchstick lay on the floor, right in the angle where the door met the jamb.

Longarm spotted it before he got to the door and never broke stride. Instead, he walked on past Room Fifteen and went all the way down the hall to the narrow set of side stairs. Anyone listening inside his room would think that he was some other late-arriving guest.

With surprising grace for a man of his size, Longarm cat-footed back up the hall to his door, being careful not to let any of the floorboards squeak underneath him. He paused just outside the room and listened intently.

Not hearing a sound, he bent to look closely at the doorknob and lock. He was certain he had turned the key in the lock when he left, so whoever had gotten inside the room must have either persuaded Joel Guthrie to let him in or stolen an extra key.

Or picked the lock, and that was what Longarm was checking for now. He had heard of cracksmen back East who could open a door with a bent piece of metal and never leave a mark, but he figured the odds of someone like that being in Panamint were pretty slim.

The lock didn't have any scratches around it. That left getting a key from Guthrie.

Longarm suddenly stiffened as he realized that he hadn't even glanced behind the desk when he came through the lobby. Guthrie could have been back there, knocked out or even murdered.

Longarm backed silently away from the door. He went downstairs just as quietly, drawing his gun along the way.

The lobby still appeared to be deserted. He went to the desk and leaned over to look behind it.

Nothing. No body, no blood, no signs of a struggle.

"You're gettin' a mite worrisome in your old age, Custis," he muttered to himself.

There was nothing left to do now except take matters into his own hands. He went upstairs again, not attempting to be quiet this time. He kept his Colt in his hand as he walked along the hall. He even whistled a little tune as he approached the door of Room Fifteen.

The old hymn, "Further Along We'll Know More About It" . . .

When he reached the door, he slid the key in the lock, turned it, swiftly grasped the knob, and twisted. He shoved the door open.

And went in fast behind it in a rolling dive that saw him come up on one knee, gun in hand, ready to fire.

Chapter 12

"Oh, my God!" Dr. Amelia Judd gasped in shock as she leaped up from the chair where she'd been sitting.

Longarm bit back a curse and lowered his .44. "Pardon my language, Doc," he said as he rose to his feet, "but what in blue blazes are you doin' in my room?"

"I heard you were almost killed," she said. "I came over to make sure you weren't hurt."

Longarm pouched his iron. "I'm fine, if you don't count figurin' I was about to get bushwhacked again. Who told you about the shootin'?"

"Mr. Guthrie. I heard the shots and thought that my services might be needed. Unfortunately, Mr. Horne was in the middle of another bout of sickness, so I couldn't check on them right away. I came as soon as I could, though."

"How come Guthrie didn't tell you I was all right? He knew I'd just gone over to the café to get somethin' to eat."

Dr. Judd looked away and didn't meet Longarm's eyes. "He did say that. I just . . . wanted to be sure."

"So you asked him to let you into my room so you could wait for me?"

"That's right."

He sensed that something else was going on here, but he wasn't sure what it was.

The best way to find out, he supposed, would be to play along with her.

He took off his hat, hung it on the bedpost, and smiled at her. "Well, as you can see for yourself, I'm fine."

She let her gaze play over him with a physician's frankness. "Yes, I can see that," she said. "You appear to be the picture of robust vitality, Marshal."

Longarm suppressed the urge to chuckle. "I reckon you could say that."

"You weren't injured at all during the exchange of gunfire?"

"Nope."

She came a step closer to him. "Have you experienced any other symptoms? Any weakness or the urgent need to evacuate your bowels?"

This time he couldn't stop himself from laughing. "I do believe you're the first lady to ever ask me that question, Doc. The prettiest one, for sure."

She blushed. "I'm not a lady," she said. "I'm a doctor. Although . . . I wouldn't mind if you were to call me Amelia, rather than . . . Doc."

"I reckon I can do that," Longarm agreed with a nod. "And to answer your question, Amelia, I'm fine. Nary a twinge anywhere. The only problem I've had with my belly lately is that it was plumb empty earlier, but I took care of that with a surroundin' at Cletus Donnelly's Café."

She smiled back at him. "Yes, Mr. Donnelly is a fine cook, isn't he?"

Longarm asked a question of his own. "Has anybody else come down sick yet?"

"Not so far, thank goodness. But I'm afraid it's only a matter of time."

"How much time?"

Amelia shook her head. "That's impossible to say. It depends on how potent this strain of the disease is. It would be an absolute miracle, though, if Mr. Horne were the only one affected."

"Yeah, I figured that would be too much to hope for. I guess we'll just have to ride out the storm, however long it lasts."

She came closer still. "Yes, but it doesn't hurt to have someone to ... ride it out with, I suppose you could say."

Longarm had been puzzled by the look in her eyes, but now he recognized it for what it was.

Amelia was hot and bothered. She might not want to be, but she was anyway.

"Don't you need to be gettin' back to your house so you can keep an eye on Horne?" asked Longarm.

She shook her head. "He's sleeping again now. Anyway, I left Tim there with him. He serves as my assistant whenever I need him to."

"Tim? I figured him for a prospector or a mill worker."

"He worked in one of the mines for a while, but he suffers from, well, I suppose you'd call it a nerve condition. He can't stand to be in enclosed places. He can barely force himself to stay in his cabin. I told him to go home earlier tonight, you may recall, but I found him wandering around my front yard not long after that. He'll check in on Mr. Horne from time to time."

Longarm found that pretty interesting, because Tim was one of the people he suspected of being the varmint who'd busted into his room and started shooting.

Tim might have a grudge against him because of that ruckus they'd had earlier in the livery barn. Longarm really couldn't think of anybody else in Panamint who'd go to so much trouble to blow out his candle, unless . . .

Unless it was Gideon Horne.

The thought caused Longarm's breath to hiss between his teeth. Amelia frowned and asked, "What is it?"

"This is gonna sound like a stupid question, Doc . . . I mean Amelia."

"Is it about medicine?" She smiled. "Because if it is, there are no stupid questions."

"Yeah, it is. Is there any chance that Horne ain't really as sick as it seems he is?"

Amelia stared at him. "You mean . . . could he be *faking* cholera?" She shook her head. "That's absolutely impossible, Marshal. In the first place, no one would do such a thing, and in the second, the symptoms are unmistakable. No, Mr. Horne is a very, very sick man and may not even survive until morning. Why would you think otherwise?"

"I was just checkin' on something. The fella who busted into the room down the hall where I was earlier and started shootin' at me used two handguns." Longarm's mind went back to that bloody night at Mama Lupe's in El Paso when the outlaw had gunned down Bert Collins. "Horne's a two-gun man."

"That may well be true, but I promise you, he wasn't up gallivanting around Panamint and . . . and ambushing you earlier tonight. It's utterly impossible."

"Well, I reckon I can rule that out, then."

"I imagine that in your line of work, you get shot at on occasion."

A wry grin curved the big lawman's mouth under the sweeping longhorn mustache. "A heap more often than I care to think about," he acknowledged.

"Being a doctor is dangerous, too."

"I'm sure it is. You're exposed to all sorts of contagion."

"Yes, plus there's the strain of sometimes having people's lives in your hands. I suspect you know about that, too."

Longarm nodded. "Yeah, that's true."

She had moved even closer to him, until now she was only about a foot away. Her head tipped back a little so she could look up into his face.

"People who live on the edge of death have to seize life whenever they have a chance, don't they?" she whispered.

"That's sort of the way I've always looked at it."

She put a slender hand on his chest. "Marshal Long—"

"Custis."

She nodded. "Custis, I know this is awfully brazen of me, but I could use a bit of . . . comfort . . . tonight."

"I'm sure you ain't the only one in Panamint who feels that way, Amelia."

Dallas Farrar, for example, he thought.

"I know I'm not," Amelia said. "But I'm the only one who's here right now with you."

"Now that is mighty true," said Longarm as he brought a hand up and cupped it on the back of her neck. He leaned forward and kissed her.

She put her hands on his chest, not to shove him away but rather to clutch at him as their mouths melded together. Her body surged urgently against his. Longarm slid his other arm around her waist and pulled her tightly to him.

It was a good kiss, hot and sweet and passionate. It left both of them wanting more, much more.

Longarm didn't want to rush things, though. He pulled back and said, "Are you sure about this, Amelia?"

"I've never been more sure about anything in my life," she said breathlessly.

Longarm smiled. "All right, then." The fingers of one hand went to the buttons of her blouse. "I reckon we can oblige each other."

He unfastened the buttons and peeled back the blouse, exposing her breasts in a thin shift. The nipples were erect and poked enticingly against the fabric. Longarm cupped the left breast and ran his thumb over the bud of hard, pebbled flesh.

Amelia shivered and put her hand on top of Longarm's hand, pressing it harder into the mound. "You don't have to be gentle with me, Custis," she whispered. "In fact . . . I'd really rather you weren't."

He took her at her word and quickly stripped her of her clothes, not roughly but efficiently. While her body had been covered up, he hadn't realized what a lovely shape she really had. Her creamy skin was smooth and sleek, and against its paleness, the triangle of hair where her thighs came together seemed even darker.

Longarm let his hands roam all over her body. She seemed to like it and cried out softly a few times when he explored her most intimate areas. She clutched at his arms and thrust her hips forward as he reached between her legs and slipped a finger into her.

She was already wet, and it slid easily between the folds of her sex. The interior muscles tightened hotly around his finger, especially when he used his thumb to stroke the hard little nubbin at the top of her opening.

"Oh, my God, Custis," she gasped. "That feels so good." Her hands pawed at the front of his denim trousers. "You have to let me . . . do something for you."

"That would be mighty fine," he told her. He slid his finger in and out of her a few more times, then took it out so that she could drop to her knees in front of him.

He unbuckled his gun belt and set it on the chair. Meanwhile, Amelia was working at his regular belt and his fly. She got everything undone and hauled it down, trousers, long underwear, and all.

Longarm's cock sprang free, bobbing a little in the open air. On her knees, Amelia leaned back and eyed it in surprise.

"I had a feeling that you'd be well endowed, Custis, but I must say, that's the largest male member I think I've ever seen. Speaking as a doctor, of course." She looked up at him. "Speaking as a woman, I'm not at all sure I can get that monster inside me."

"But you're willin' to try, I imagine."

"Oh, yes," Amelia said. "More than willing."

As if to prove that, she leaned forward again and grasped the shaft with both hands as she opened her mouth and closed her lips around the head. The warm, wet oral caress sent a throb of pleasure through Longarm.

Amelia sucked gently on the head while she stroked the shaft with her palms. Her tongue circled hotly around the crown. Longarm felt the urge to thrust deeper into her mouth but suppressed it. He didn't want to choke her.

Instead he took the pins out of her upswept hair and let the mass of dark curls tumble around her shoulders. That made her even more beautiful as far as he was concerned.

Even though what she was doing to him was exquisite, there was only so much of it he could take without exploding into her mouth, and he didn't want to do that.

So finally he reached down and took hold of her shoulders, urging her up. He was going to sweep her up and put her on the bed, but she took care of that herself, turning away from him and climbing onto the mattress.

She grabbed the pillow and pulled it under her head

as she lifted her butt into the air. "This is the way . . . I like it," she forced out in a voice husky and strained with need. "I hope that's . . . all right with you."

Longarm looked at the beautiful sight displayed before him—the pale columns of her thighs, the smooth, rounded globes of her buttocks, the tight, puckered brown opening between them, and the dark pink folds below that shined with her copious juices—and wasn't about to complain.

"I reckon that's fine and dandy," he told her.

"Then fuck me!" Amelia urged. "Fuck me hard!"

Again, Longarm wasn't going to argue. Without even pausing to take his shirt off or finish removing his trousers and long underwear, he positioned himself behind her and drove his cock into her, sheathing it all the way with one forceful thrust.

Amelia breathed, "Ohhhhh," in a voice rich with satisfaction.

Longarm dug his fingers into her hips and started pistoning in and out of her, hard and fast. With each thrust, he stretched the tight confines of her sex. He saw her fingers flexing on the pillow as he filled her.

She was so hot, wet, and eager that he knew he might not last long. But he didn't think she would either. She thrust back against him, matching him thrust for thrust.

After a couple of minutes, she gasped, "Your finger! Put your finger in . . . in . . ."

She couldn't find the breath to finish the entreaty, but Longarm knew what she wanted.

He reached between them, dipped the middle finger of his right hand into her honeypot alongside his shaft to get it good and wet, then took it out and speared it into the tight passage just above her pussy.

Amelia bucked and cried out, but not in pain. "Oh, yes, oh, yes!" she urged. "Just like that! Just like that!"

Longarm continued the double penetration, delving as deep into both holes as he could. Amelia began to spasm as her climax gripped her, so Longarm let go as well and surged into her one last time as his juices exploded from him.

It was a long, timeless moment as the two of them shared the greatest intimacy a man and a woman could share. Longarm stayed buried within her until she moaned and all her muscles went limp at once. She slumped forward onto the bed as his cock and his finger slid out of her.

Longarm stretched out on the mattress beside her. She rolled toward him and put an arm around his neck as she buried her face against his chest. He could feel her heart slugging heavily behind the breast that flattened against him.

"That was . . . amazing," Amelia said when she had caught her breath enough to talk again. "The sort of thing . . . that a woman will never forget . . . no matter how long she lives."

Longarm wondered if that was a reference to the danger they all faced. Earlier tonight, he had bedded Dallas because she wanted to experience that passion one more time. Amelia might be feeling the same thing.

After a moment, she patted his broad, muscular chest and said, "I have to go."

"You're welcome to stay the night," he told her.

"I know, but I have a responsibility to my patient."

"Gideon Horne's a low-down, murderin' owlhoot. I wouldn't lose a lot of sleep over an hombre like him, Amelia."

She smiled at him. "Maybe you'd better call me Doc again, because I *am* still a doctor, you know."

"I know. And I reckon I understand."

She leaned over him and gave him a long, lingering

kiss before whispering, "Good night, Custis."

"Good night . . . Doc."

She dressed quickly and left. For the second time to-night, Longarm got out of his clothes, except for his long underwear, blew out the lamp, and climbed into bed. Dawn couldn't be very many hours away by now, but he wanted to get what sleep he could in the meantime.

Even though that stubborn sense of something being wrong that he couldn't quite see still nagged at him, this time he dozed off.

His last thought was that maybe he'd be able to figure it all out in the morning.

Chapter 13

Instead, he woke up to an unexpected sound drifting in through the open window. As he forced his eyes open, the intensity of the light in the room told him that the sun was up. He had slept longer than he meant to.

Then his eyes opened wider and he sat up as he realized what he was hearing.

Somebody out there was blowing a cavalry bugle.

Longarm swung his legs out of bed and stood up. He hurried over to the window, thrust the curtains aside, and lifted the pane high enough that he could stick his head and shoulders out and look around.

The bugle notes were coming from the end of town where he had ridden in the night before. The bugler wasn't actually *in* town, though, Longarm saw. The man sat his horse about a hundred yards from the lower end of Main Street. Another mounted, blue-uniformed cavalryman was beside him.

And another hundred yards beyond them was an entire mounted patrol of a couple of dozen men, obviously waiting for some response from the settlement.

Longarm grabbed his clothes and pulled them on. He

didn't know what was going on here, but he wanted to find out.

When he was dressed, he left the room and clattered down the stairs to the lobby. Joel Guthrie was behind the desk, looking worried and puzzled.

"Marshal, do you have any idea why the cavalry is here?" he asked.

Longarm shook his head. "Nope. But I'm on my way to ask those soldier boys right now."

As he strode out into the street, he took stock of his condition this morning. He didn't feel any unusual rumblings in his stomach or bowels. His guts seemed to be perfectly normal.

So far, so good, he thought. No cholera.

Mayor McQuiddy hurried toward him from the direction of Donnelly's Café. The mayor had probably been having breakfast when he heard the insistent blaring of the bugle.

"What is it, Marshal?" he called to Longarm.

"Don't know," Longarm said again.

"But . . . but why is the cavalry here?"

Longarm nodded toward the riders. "Let's go ask 'em."

He started toward the two cavalrymen closest to the settlement. McQuiddy hurried along beside him. The mayor had to trot to keep up with the lawman's longer-legged strides.

Longarm might have slowed down to make it easier on McQuiddy, but he was as curious as anybody else. The sooner he talked to the cavalrymen, the sooner he would know what this visit was about.

Something stirred inside him, but it was a hunch that he might not like the answer to, not the illness that had laid low Gideon Horne that had his gut uneasy.

More people were on the street this morning, although Panamint still didn't resemble the boomtown it was supposed to be. A lot of the citizens were probably staying close to home because of the cholera scare.

Some of the townspeople followed Longarm and McQuiddy, though, so there was a small group by the time they passed Dr. Amelia Judd's house.

Amelia came out on the porch and raised a hand to shade her eyes against the morning sunlight. She hurried down the walk to the fence gate, opened it, and came toward Longarm.

"Custis, what's all this?" she asked. A wry smile touched her lips. "A parade?"

"Not hardly," said Longarm. "Although we got a fella playin' the bugle out there."

As a matter of fact, the bugler had fallen silent. Longarm guessed that was because he had seen the group coming toward him and knew that his music had done its intended job.

"Are you going to talk to them?" Amelia asked.

"That's right."

She fell in step alongside him and declared, "Then I'm coming with you."

"Fine by me. How's Horne this mornin'?"

"Still alive. That's really more than I expected. I still don't think that he'll recover, though."

The three of them in the forefront of the group from Panamint were approaching the cavalrymen. Longarm could see now that the second man was an officer, wearing a gray hat with the crossed sabers insignia of the cavalry rather than a black campaign cap like the bugler.

The officer held up a hand in a signal to halt when Longarm, Amelia, and McQuiddy were still about forty feet from him.

"That's close enough," he called. "You folks stay right there, not a step closer."

Longarm raised his voice and asked, "Who are you? What's this about?"

"I'm Captain Jason Shaw, in command of this detachment from Fort Winston. Are you someone in authority, sir?"

"Deputy U.S. Marshal Long," replied Longarm. He nodded to the man beside him. "This is A.P. McQuiddy, the mayor of Panamint. What brings you fellas here?"

Captain Shaw rested his hands on his saddle and leaned forward, his face grim in the morning light. "Cholera."

Amelia gasped in surprise, and McQuiddy muttered a curse. Longarm kept his own face impassive as he said, "What are you talkin' about, Captain?"

Shaw jerked a hand in a curt gesture and snapped, "Let's not beat around the bush, Marshal. The army is aware that there's a cholera outbreak in Panamint. We've been sent here to do something about it."

"What can you do about it?" Amelia demanded. "You're soldiers, not doctors."

Shaw regarded her coolly as he said, "And who are you, ma'am, if you don't mind me asking?"

Amelia's chin lifted in defiance. "Dr. Amelia Judd," she said. "I'm the only physician in Panamint."

"Then you know how dangerous cholera is."

"We've been doing our best to contain it—"

"That's our job now," Shaw cut in.

"What do you mean by that, Captain?" asked Longarm.

"No one goes in or out of Panamint until the disease has run its course and is no longer a threat. My men and I are here to enforce that quarantine."

McQuiddy sputtered, "But . . . but you can't—"

"Yes, we can, Mayor. The town is now under martial law."

"We've been trying to keep anyone from leaving," Amelia said. "We don't want the disease to spread."

"Well, you haven't done a good enough job of it," Shaw snapped. "A freighter who passed through here arrived at the fort a couple of days ago and fell sick almost immediately. He died in a matter of hours, but not before telling us that the last place he stopped was in Panamint. He had to have brought the disease from here."

"But that's not possible," Amelia objected. "We thought the carrier was a newcomer here, a man named Horne."

"You thought wrong," Shaw said. "The post surgeon identified the disease that killed the freighter as cholera and said that he must have been infected here."

Amelia frowned. "Then it was lurking here before Horne even arrived," she mused. "I never dreamed . . ." She looked up at Shaw. "What did you do with the man who died at the fort, Captain?"

"We burned his wagon and everything in it," Shaw replied harshly. "Including the freighter's body."

"Good Lord," said McQuiddy.

"It was an extreme measure, I know," Shaw said with a nod, "but our commanding officer ordered it to make certain that the disease didn't spread any further." He paused, "There was some discussion about whether or not we should burn Panamint to make sure of the same thing."

"Burn Panamint!" McQuiddy yelped. "You can't—"

The cavalry officer held up a gauntleted hand to forestall McQuiddy's protest. "It was decided that wouldn't be necessary. But a quarantine is."

Longarm looked over at Amelia. "What do you think, Doc?"

She chewed at her lower lip for a second as she thought

about it. "We were already trying to keep the disease isolated here in town," she said. "The way I see it, making it official doesn't really change anything."

"I don't like it," said McQuiddy. "The army's acting like it's our fault."

"Well, clearly the cholera *did* come from here," Amelia said. "Horne didn't bring it in like we thought."

"But why is he the only one who's gotten sick? I don't understand."

"Neither do I, Mr. Mayor," Amelia replied with a faint smile. "Disease is a capricious thing. Sometimes it strikes down one and not the other."

McQuiddy looked at Shaw. "How long do we have to stay bottled up, Captain?"

"My orders are to evaluate the situation in a week and decide on a further course of action then."

"But you're not a doctor," Amelia challenged him. "How are you going to make such a decision?"

Shaw smiled. "It's a good thing *you're* here, Doctor, because I intend to rely heavily on your knowledge and advice. In the end, though, the decision *will* be mine."

McQuiddy looked at Longarm and asked, "What can we do except go along with him, Marshal? He's got a whole patrol of soldiers out there."

"Yeah, that's about the size of it," Longarm agreed.

"It just feels like . . . I don't know, like they're laying siege to the town or something!"

Longarm nodded. "That's what it amounts to, I reckon." He raised his voice again and addressed Shaw. "Just out of curiosity, Captain . . . if somebody tries to leave town, what are you gonna do to them?"

"My orders are clear, Marshal," Shaw replied. "If anyone attempts to leave, my men will order them to turn back."

"And if they don't?"

"Then my men will shoot," said Shaw. "And they have orders to shoot to kill."

Since there was obviously nothing to be gained from further discussion with the captain, Longarm, Amelia, and McQuiddy turned back toward Panamint. The mayor shooed the townspeople along in front and told them to go on about their business.

The group buzzed with excited, nervous conversation. Within a half hour, Longarm knew, everybody in town would have heard about the cavalry and the quarantine they had come to enforce, and what would happen if anyone tried to leave.

Since there was nothing he could do at the moment, Longarm headed for Donnelly's Café, intent on getting some breakfast.

He hadn't forgotten about the attempt on his life the night before. He couldn't rule out Tim as the would-be killer, but it seemed unlikely he could prove anything one way or the other.

Whoever had taken those shots at him, he didn't think the varmint would try again in broad daylight, in the middle of town. Especially now that the army was just outside of town.

Of course, he might be wrong about that, he reminded himself, so he'd keep a close eye out, as usual.

Amelia went back in her house, but McQuiddy walked on to the café with Longarm. "I don't have much of an appetite anymore," he said, "but I suppose it would be a good idea to keep my strength up, just in case I get sick."

"Yeah, I reckon so," Longarm agreed, adding, "That's my plan anyway."

The second breakfast Longarm ate in a matter of hours was as good as the first. If anything, he thought as he washed down Cletus Donnelly's excellent grub, his appetite was even better than usual, and he felt fine despite not getting much sleep.

The fact that he'd had some mighty fine lovin' from two beautiful women the night before might have something to do with that, he told himself with a smile. Nothing invigorated an hombre more than a good romp in the hay, unless it was two romps in the hay, even when there was no actual hay involved.

The same worried hush that had been prevalent the night before still hung over Panamint this morning. For the most part, people stayed off the streets, and when they did come out, they hurried through whatever chore they were about, looking around nervously all the while.

Everybody was so scared, in fact, that it was like the whole town was sitting on a giant powder keg, just waiting for the lit fuse that was burning closer and closer to finally reach its destination.

Then everything would blow sky-high, thought Longarm.

It was up to him, McQuiddy, and Amelia to keep that from happening.

Things got worse around the middle of the day. Longarm was sitting on a bench in front of the hotel, smoking a cheroot, when he spotted Tim hurrying along the boardwalk toward him.

The big lawman's hand instinctively moved a little closer to his gun, but he didn't draw the Colt. He didn't trust Tim, and judging by the churlish expression on the man's face, he didn't have any reason to.

Tim stopped on the hotel porch and jerked a thumb over his shoulder. "The doctor wants to see you," he said.

Longarm stood up and took the cheroot out of his mouth. "What about?"

"Don't know," Tim replied with a shake of his head. "She didn't tell me. Just said to find you and fetch you."

"All right." Longarm nodded. "I'm obliged." He paused before he started toward Amelia's house. "How are you doin', Tim?"

Judging by the sudden frown on the man's rawboned face, the question surprised Tim. "What do you mean?" he asked suspiciously. "Do I look like I'm comin' down with that sickness or somethin'?"

"Just an innocent question," Longarm said.

"Well, I'm fine, I reckon, not that it's any damned business of yours."

"All right. I'm glad to hear it."

Longarm remembered the splashes of blood on the floor of the hotel room. He had wounded the man who'd broken in and tried to kill him. Tim appeared to be un-hurt. Of course, it was possible for a man to conceal a wound, but Longarm had a hunch that wasn't the case here.

Short of drawing his gun and forcing Tim to strip down to the buff, he couldn't prove that the man didn't have any bullet holes in him. For now, though, Longarm leaned toward the theory that Tim wasn't the gunman who'd tried to kill him.

That left the question of who had.

Longarm didn't have an answer.

Even so, he didn't much cotton to the idea of turning his back on Tim. He did it anyway, heading down the street toward Amelia's place.

Nobody bothered him along the way. When he got there, he found Amelia alone sitting in a rocking chair on the front porch. He could tell from the expression on her face that something was very wrong. He went up a couple of steps and stopped with one foot on the porch.

"What is it?" he asked.

She looked up at him with a dull, defeated expression in her eyes. "Mr. Horne died a short time ago," she said.

Longarm put the cheroot in his mouth and clamped his teeth down hard on it.

Rest in peace, Bert, he thought. *The son of a bitch who put you under has crossed the divide. Might not have been the law that caught up to him, but he's shakin' hands with the Devil right about now either way. And he died mighty hard, too.*

"You figured he wasn't gonna make it," Longarm said around the gasper.

"Yes, of course," Amelia agreed, "but still, a doctor always hates to lose a patient, no matter how hopeless the situation is. And no matter what sort of a man that patient was either."

"Well, don't lose much sleep over Horne," Longarm said. "He ain't worth it. You already done a lot more for him than he deserved."

Amelia shrugged. "Perhaps."

Longarm took the cheroot out of his mouth and blew a smoke ring.

"Here's what I'm worried about," he said. "When word gets around town that Horne's dead, it's just gonna make folks more scared than ever. They probably wouldn't admit it, but a part of 'em had to be hopin' that he'd pull through, that things ain't really as bad as what they appear to be. They were already pretty much scared out of their skin."

"But now they'll know for sure just how deadly the disease is," Amelia said, nodding slowly. "You're right, Custis. It already feels like a storm is about to break over Panamint, and this will just make it worse. If anything else happens . . ."

"If anything else happens, we're liable to have a stampede," Longarm finished the thought for her. "And with a bunch of nervous cavalrymen out there with orders to shoot to kill, it'll be like all hell breakin' loose . . ."

Chapter 14

Something had to be done with Horne's body. Longarm found McQuiddy in the hardware store that the mayor owned and broke the news of the outlaw's death.

McQuiddy didn't look relieved.

"Let's go see if Joe Carswell wants to take care of the burial," he suggested. "Joe's our undertaker."

"Reckon he should be used to such things," said Longarm.

"Not cholera," McQuiddy said with a shake of his head. "Nobody gets used to cholera."

Longarm supposed the mayor had a point about that.

A few minutes later, in the back room of the undertaking parlor, Joe Carswell shook his head emphatically.

"No, sir," he declared. "I don't want to have anything to do with that body. I don't care what you do with it, but don't bring it anywhere near here."

"But that's your job, Joe," McQuiddy argued. "You've buried folks who died of illness before, many times."

"Yeah, but never any that had anything like cholera. I'm sorry, A.P., but I just can't do it. No sir, I won't do it. I got a wife and kids. I can't risk it."

"Dr. Judd says that Horne was around so many people before he came down sick that the whole town's been exposed, either directly or indirectly. The danger's already here."

"Maybe so, but there's no point in making it even worse," Carswell said stubbornly. "I will not do it."

McQuiddy sighed and looked over at Longarm. "What will we do, Marshal?"

"You have any coffins already nailed together out back, Mr. Carswell?" Longarm asked.

Carswell shrugged and admitted, "Well, yeah, I do. There's a couple out there."

"If you'll loan me your wagon and a shovel, I'll take care of the chore."

"You can have the coffin, I guess. I don't even care if I get paid for it. But you can't use my wagon, it stays here. I don't want it anywhere near that corpse."

"I have a wagon," McQuiddy said with disgust. "We'll use it, Marshal. And I have plenty of shovels at the store, too, of course."

Longarm nodded. "All right. We'd better get at it. The day'll get even hotter before it cools off again."

A short time later, they pulled the wagon up at the rear of Amelia's house. Longarm and McQuiddy went inside and found that Amelia had already wrapped Gideon Horne's body in a sheet, although she had left the outlaw's face uncovered for the time being. More than twenty-four hours of hellish suffering had etched deep lines in Horne's hollow cheeks.

"Ain't nobody gonna be mournin' you, old son," Longarm said as he looked down at the body, "and I hope you're roastin' in hell right now. But no matter what you done, we'll lay your earthly remains to rest proper-like."

He pulled the sheet over Horne's face, thinking as he

did so that now no one would ever know where that loot from the train robbery was stashed. Some lucky hombre might come across it one of these days, or it might be lost for all time.

Longarm and McQuiddy placed the sheeted body in the coffin. Then they carried the coffin out the back door of Amelia's house and placed it on the ground in the shade of a tree. Using a hammer and a keg of nails they had also brought from the mayor's store, Longarm nailed the lid down securely.

Once that was done, it was just a matter of driving up to Panamint's Boot Hill cemetery and digging a grave.

Longarm was hot and tired by the time they were finished with that chore, but he was relieved to throw the last shovelful of dirt back onto the mound of earth that marked Gideon Horne's final resting place.

"There you go, old son," he said as he stepped back and leaned on the shovel to rest for a moment. "Enjoy eternity burnin' in hell."

"You *really* disliked that fellow, didn't you, Marshal?" McQuiddy asked. He had removed his coat and rolled up his sleeves to do his share of the spade work.

"He gunned down a fine lawman, and from what I know of the rest of his life, he never did any good for anybody else. Plus he did his damnedest to kill me, too, and came mighty close to accomplishin' that goal a couple times." Longarm regarded the grave for a moment and added, "Still and all, I'd have rather seen him hanged or put a slug through him my own self. Dyin' the way he did . . . that's a bad way to go."

McQuiddy grunted. "Are there any *good* ways to go?"

A grin stretched across Longarm's sweaty face. "The Indians claim it's good to die in battle against your enemies. So do other folks that us *civilized* people would call barbarians. Sometimes I think they're a heap smarter than

us. One thing's for sure . . . it's the barbarians who're
likely gonna win in the end."

"The ultimate triumph, eh?" mused McQuiddy. "You
may be right, Marshal. I think I'd like to hold on to civi-
lization for a while longer, though."

"That's what they pay me for," said Longarm as he
tossed the shovel into the back of the wagon. He climbed
onto the driver's seat as McQuiddy threw his shovel in
the back and sat next to Longarm in the wagon.

From up here on Boot Hill, Longarm could see the
cavalry troops that had surrounded Panamint. The company had set up a camp several hundred yards outside of
the settlement. Two-man patrols were riding a constant
circuit to make sure no one tried to leave town . . . keeping a safe distance away, of course.

Even at this distance, Longarm recognized Jason Shaw
as the captain strode from one of the tents that had been
set up to another. Shaw walked with a slight limp, so it
was a good thing he was in the cavalry and could spend
most of his time in the saddle, Longarm reflected.

McQuiddy took up the reins and drove back to the
store. Longarm dropped off the wagon before they got
there, saying, "I'll see you later, Mayor."

He headed toward the Copper Queen, passing the
town's public well as he did so. Longarm paused beside it.

After doing most of the work of digging that grave
and covering it back up again, he was hot and thirsty. A
bucket was attached to a windlass over the well, and a
dipper hung on a nail on the windlass frame.

Longarm still planned to get something to drink at
the saloon, but some nice, cool water right now might
help quench his thirst. He loosened the bucket and lowered it.

The well had been sunk deep in the earth. In these
parts, you had to go deep to avoid the alkali and other

minerals. It was almost half a minute before he heard the faint splash of the bucket hitting water.

He let it fill and cranked it back up. When he filled the dipper and took a drink, he found the water to be cold and good-tasting. Longarm drank all of it from the dipper and poured the rest from the bucket back into the well.

Wiping the back of his hand across his mouth, he turned toward the Copper Queen.

The saloon was doing good business today, he saw as he shouldered through the batwings, but even though there were quite a few customers here, the place was eerily quiet. No one was playing cards. Men stood at the bar or sat at the tables drinking, barely talking to each other.

Often in perilous situations, some men would develop a false sense of bravado, Longarm knew. They would be more boisterous than usual, laughing and talking and making jokes.

But most men, when they thought they were staring death in the face, grew quiet. They might drink, as these men were doing, but it didn't make them drunk. They guzzled whiskey in hopes of numbing their fear.

But some fears were too strong even for whiskey to overcome.

All eyes turned toward Longarm when he came in. Dallas Farrar stood at the end of the bar, looking lovely in a dark blue gown.

She would have been even prettier without the dark circles under her eyes that showed she hadn't slept much the night before.

She came over to Longarm and rested a hand on his arm. No one in the saloon was talking now. They were just watching quietly.

"We heard that that outlaw, that man Horne, died a while ago," Dallas said. "Is that true, Custis?"

Longarm wasn't going to lie to her. He nodded and said, "That's right. Mayor McQuiddy and I just took his body up to Boot Hill and buried it."

"I . . . I know it's crazy, but I thought . . . I hoped if maybe he pulled through, there'd be some hope for the rest of us . . ."

"There ain't no hope," a man said, his voice harsh in the hush of the room. "We're all gonna die. It's just a matter of time."

Longarm turned sharply toward him. "You think so?" he snapped. "How do you feel right now, mister?"

The man looked surprised at the big lawman's reaction. "Me?" he said. "Why, I . . . I reckon I'm fine. Right now. Just worried, that's all."

"You're more than worried. You're scared." Longarm let the pent-up anger lash out in his voice as he turned his head to look all around the room. "All of you are scared to death."

"We got every right to be!" another man responded hotly. "That stuff'll kill you!"

A grizzled old-timer in buckskins came to his feet. "I done fought Injuns and outlaws and all kinds of bad weather!" he declared. "Nobody calls me a coward, goldurn it! But sickness like that . . . hell, you can't even see it! How in blazes is anybody supposed to fight it?"

"They have a point, Custis," Dallas said softly.

"Maybe," said Longarm. He swept an arm to take in the entire room. "But who in here is sick right now?"

Silence was the only answer to his question.

"Anybody?" Longarm persisted. "Anybody feelin' puny? Feel like you need to run to the outhouse?"

The men in the saloon just stared at him and didn't say anything.

After a minute, Longarm grunted. "That's what I thought. You're all as healthy as horses."

Dallas clutched at his arm. "But Custis, how can that be?" she wanted to know. "Horne *died*. You saw his body yourself."

"That's true," Longarm admitted.

"And that cavalry captain said a freighter who came through here got sick and died at Fort Winston. He must have gotten the disease here. We had it among us all along. Horne didn't bring it with him."

"No, Horne didn't bring the cholera here. But if it was as bad as everybody seems to think, wouldn't more people be sick by now? Wouldn't more people be dead or dying?"

Dallas frowned and looked confused, as did most of the men in the room. None of them could argue with the logic of what Longarm had just said.

"But if you're right, Custis, how do you explain Horne and that freighter?" asked Dallas.

"I can't . . . yet," Longarm said. "But I'm not gonna curl up and wait to die just because there's a chance I *might* get sick."

"You're right." A new intensity began to burn in Dallas's eyes. "You're right, Custis." She turned and threw an arm out. "Drinks on the house, boys!"

Normally an announcement like that would have brought a cheer from the customers. Not today. Several of the men did mutter their appreciation, though.

Dallas said to a slick-haired gent who sat at a table near the piano, "Sam, go tickle those ivories."

"Dallas, I'm not sure anybody's in the mood for music—"

"I said play, Sam!"

The man shrugged his narrow shoulders, got up, and

went over to perch on the stool in front of the piano. He started off slow, but the notes soon picked up their pace.

Dallas picked up a deck of cards from one of the tables and fanned them, then shuffled and cut them. "Get a game going, boys," she said to the men sitting there. She smiled at them. "Big winner gets to dance with me later."

The buckskin-clad oldster held up a hand and asked, "Can I get in on that?"

Dallas nudged a man's shoulder with her elbow. "Shove over there, Lew, and make room for Woody."

Slowly but surely, the noise level began to build in the room. Dallas turned to Longarm and said, "Well? Is that more like it, Custis?"

He chuckled. "It sure is. Sounds like a saloon in here again. Now if I can get me one of those drinks on the house you were talkin' about a minute ago . . ."

She grabbed his hand. "Later," she said. "You've got something else to do first."

She led him up the stairs to her room.

Longarm didn't try to get away.

Once the door was closed behind them, Dallas came into his arms and lifted her face to his for a kiss. Maybe there was still a little bit of the sad desperation from the night before in her actions, thought Longarm, but not much.

The impression he got of her now was of a hot-blooded woman who knew what she wanted and didn't mind going after it boldly.

Bold enough, in fact, that she had wiggled out of her clothes in no time flat and had already gone to work on his.

When she had him naked, too, she lay back on the bed and spread her legs wide. The triangle of auburn hair at the juncture of her thighs was enticing. Longarm knelt and brought his mouth to the entrance between her

legs. Her sex was already wet, but it grew wetter still as
he kissed and licked the folds, then thrust his tongue
between them.

Dallas hissed in pleasure and clutched at his head,
tangling her fingers in his dark hair. Longarm kept going, adding his fingers to what his lips and tongue were
doing. He explored every bit of her most intimate places
and drove her farther and farther up the pinnacle of lust
that had sprung up inside her.

Finally she broke, spasming and driving her drenched
pussy against his face. Her thighs clamped hard around
his head as her hips bucked up from the mattress. Longarm hung on tight until the last of the delicious shudders
had rolled through her.

Dallas's breasts rose and fell rapidly as she tried to
catch her breath. Grinning, Longarm climbed onto the
bed beside her and stretched out. He fondled the soft
mound nearest to him, which prompted her to reach over
somewhat blindly in search of his manhood. She found
the long, thick shaft and closed her hand on it, sighing in
satisfaction.

Longarm let her toy with him for a few minutes while
she recovered her strength. Then he pulled her on top of
him. Grinning in anticipation, Dallas straddled his hips
and lowered her honeypot onto him. She was so wet that
his iron-hard erection went into her with no trouble at all.

"Oh, Lord, Custis!" she gasped as she began to bounce
a little on top of him. "You fill me up!" She leaned forward and rested her hands on his broad chest to brace
herself as her hips started pumping madly.

Longarm thrust up into her heated sheath, matching
her stroke for stroke. His hands found her apple-sized
breasts and cupped them so that his thumbs could stroke
her hard nipples and spur her on to even greater passion.

Dallas rode him at a gallop until she climaxed again.

Longarm erupted at the same moment, splashing her inside with his juices. Dallas moaned and collapsed, lying sated on his chest as he circled her with his arms and held her. Their bodies were covered with a fine sheen of sweat.

Longarm stroked her hair and her back as they caught their breath. His cock was still buried inside her, and she made no move to dislodge it. It was a sweet moment, the sort of moment that really made life worth living, Longarm reflected.

He surprised himself by dozing off. When he woke up, he didn't know how much time had passed, but Dallas was snuggled against him, her head pillowed on his shoulder, sound asleep as well.

Longarm looked at the window, saw that what little light came around the curtain was dim. Most of the day was gone, and evening was coming on again.

He took stock of his physical condition. He was rested and felt fine. No sign so far of any illness . . . and he had not only visited Horne's sickroom, he had handled the corpse and the coffin in the process of burying the man.

The last time he had seen Amelia, she had looked hale and hearty, too.

This business was getting more and more loco all the time.

For now, though, he supposed he ought to get up and check on things in town. He reached over and fondled one of Dallas's breasts until she stirred and opened her eyes. She smiled at him.

"Ready for more, Custis?" she purred.

"Maybe later," said Longarm. "It's gettin' a mite late in the day. We'd better get up for a while."

Dallas pouted a little. "Are you sure?"

"I want to see if anybody else has come down sick."

That brought her back to sobering reality. "All right," she said. "I need to clean up a little first."

Longarm knew it wouldn't hurt him to wash up either. They shared the cloth and basin of water that sat on Dallas's dressing table. Standing there like that, the two of them naked, it was awfully tempting to suggest that they wash each other, but Longarm knew if he did that, it might be another hour or more before they got out of this room.

When they were dressed, they went downstairs. The sound of piano music, talk, and laughter rose up the stairs to meet them. While the atmosphere in the Copper Queen was a little more subdued than it might have been most nights, at least it wasn't all doom and gloom anymore.

Longarm and Dallas went to the bar. She signaled to Clancy to bring over a bottle and glasses. The big, craggy-faced bartender did so and grinned at her.

"This is more like it this evenin', lass," he said.

"Yes, and I'm glad," Dallas said with a smile. She turned to Longarm. "You were right, Custis. We were fools to just give up when we heard about—"

The slap of the batwings interrupted her. Longarm looked over to see Tim stumbling into the saloon. The man's face was pale and covered with beads of sweat. As he made his way toward the bar, more and more of the customers noticed the way he looked and fell silent again.

Tim made it to the bar and leaned against it. He swallowed hard and said, "I . . . I think I need a drink. I don't . . . don't feel so good."

"Oh, my God," Dallas whispered.

Longarm turned his body so that he was between her and Tim. "You'd better get over to the doc's place, Tim," he said. "You don't look so good either."

"I'll . . . be all right," Tim forced out. "Jus' need . . . a drink—"

Before he could say anything else, he groaned and doubled over, grabbing at his belly. Men began to yell and curse and bolt up from their chairs as Tim swayed and then stumbled back a couple of steps. He wheeled around, and Longarm saw that his eyes were wide with pain and horror.

Then Tim collapsed on the sawdust-covered floor, and an awful stench filled the air as his bowels emptied themselves violently.

Chapter 15

Longarm had seen plenty of stampedes in his life, but never like the stampede that erupted in the Copper Queen at that moment. Terrified shouts rang out as men charged toward the doors like the Devil himself was after them.

And maybe they weren't far wrong at that, thought Longarm as he looked down at Tim writhing on the floor as if all the very imps of Hell were tormenting him.

Dallas's fingernails dug into the big lawman's arm through his shirtsleeve. "My God, Custis!" she exclaimed. "What are we going to do?"

"Get everybody out of here," Longarm said.

That wasn't going to be a problem. The Copper Queen was clearing out as fast as men could force their way past one another through the doors.

"You and the girls who work here get upstairs to your rooms and stay there," Longarm went on. "Clancy, you go fetch Doc Judd."

Clancy looked at Dallas. She gestured for him to do what Longarm said. Still wearing his apron, the big bartender came out from behind the hardwood, shouldered a path through the knot of frightened men still gathered in the doorway trying to get out, and started down the street toward Amelia's house.

"What about you, Custis?" asked Dallas.

"I'm gonna stay right here and keep an eye on Tim. I don't reckon there's much I can do for him, but I can keep other folks away."

"You'll be risking your life," Dallas said.

"No more so than I have been ever since I rode into Panamint. Now get upstairs."

Dallas backed up, withdrawing to the far end of the bar, and then stopped. She looked at Longarm stubbornly and said, "This is as far as I'm going."

He heard the quiver of fear in her voice, but he also saw the look of dogged determination on her face.

"All right," he told her with a little shrug. "Just keep your distance."

Dallas nodded. She told the saloon girls in their gaudy dresses to go to their rooms, and none of them argued with her. They scampered up the stairs in a hurry.

Longarm looked behind the bar. "Got a pitcher of fresh water back there anywhere?"

"There should be," Dallas said. "Look on the shelves under the bar."

Longarm went around the near end and looked, finding the pitcher on a shelf as Dallas had said. He took it back around to where Tim lay on the floor.

Tim had stopped writhing. He seemed to be only semiconscious. His mouth sagged open, and his breath rasped harshly in his throat.

Longarm knelt beside him and put a hand behind Tim's head, lifting it from the floor.

"Custis . . ." Dallas said worriedly.

"He's got to have some fluid in him to replace what he

lost," said Longarm. "That's the only way he's gonna have any chance at all to live."

With his other hand, he held the pitcher to Tim's mouth and carefully dribbled water between his lips. Some of it trickled over the sick man's chin and onto his chest, but most of it went down his throat.

All of the saloon's customers were gone by now, leaving the room eerily quiet except for Tim's moans and groans of misery. Longarm and Dallas were alone in the room with the sick man until hurried footsteps on the boardwalk and the slap of the batwings made Longarm look up.

Amelia paused just inside the entrance, a look of dismay on her face. "Tim!" she whispered. She glanced up at Longarm and said in a more normal voice, "Clancy told me what happened, but I could barely believe it. He was at my house just a short time ago, and he seemed fine."

"He was already sick when he came in here," Longarm said. "He asked for a drink, then collapsed." He lifted the pitcher so that Amelia could see it. "I've been tryin' to get some water down him. He drank a little."

She nodded. "That's the best thing anyone can do for him. The only thing, really. I'd like to get him back to my house, where I can keep an eye on him, though."

"Go find McQuiddy. See if he'll let us use his wagon again. I expect he will."

Amelia nodded toward Dallas. "*She* can do that. I need to stay with my patient."

Dallas looked like she didn't appreciate being referred to in such a dismissive tone. Her lips compressed into a narrow line.

But she nodded and said, "I'll go find the mayor, Custis."

"Thanks," Longarm said. "I'm much obliged for the help."

Even in a desperate situation such as this, he knew better than to get in the middle of any hard feelings between two beautiful women . . . especially when he had bedded both of them.

Amelia stepped aside to let Dallas leave the saloon. They cast hard glances at each other as Dallas passed her on the way out. The batwings flapped behind the owner of the Copper Queen.

Longarm gave Tim some more water as Amelia came closer. She said, "This is really bad, Custis. I expect Tim will be just the first of the townspeople to come down with the disease." Her voice rose and shook a little. "And it's just going to be worse because the army's got us all penned up together like this!"

Longarm glanced at the doors. Men were peeping over the batwings, wide-eyed with fear but driven by curiosity to see what was happening. He heard the rapid, frightened muttering among them as they reacted to what Amelia had just said.

"I thought you wanted to keep the sickness contained here," he said.

Amelia was breathing heavily now and looked terribly conflicted. "I do!" she said. "I know that medically, that's best. And yet . . . some of the townspeople probably aren't infected yet. They could be saved, if only they could get out of Panamint!"

The muttering outside became angry yelling. "The doc says we ought to get out of town!" a man shouted.

"She says some of us might live if we leave!" another man added.

Longarm set the pitcher aside and stood up. He stepped over to Amelia and put his hands on her shoulders.

"You got to pull yourself together," he told her. "Folks are ready to panic, and when they hear you talkin' like that—"

The shouts outside rose to such a crescendo that he fell silent. It was too late now for caution. The damage had already been done.

He let go of Amelia and stepped over to the batwings to peer out into the street. It was chaos out there, people yelling and running around like chickens with their heads cut off.

It wasn't just blind panic on everybody's part, though. Some of the townsmen were thinking more clearly than others. One man leaped into the back of a parked wagon and held up his hands, bellowing, "Listen to me! Listen to me! The army can't stop all of us! Get your guns! We'll shoot our way out if we have to!"

A shout of agreement went up. Men began to run, but this time they weren't just dashing about. They were headed to their homes to fetch weapons.

Longarm's face was grim as he pushed the batwings aside and strode out. Over his shoulder, he told Amelia, "Stay in there and keep an eye on Tim."

He headed for the wagon where the man was still haranguing the members of the mob who hadn't made up their minds yet. "It's our only chance! If we stay here, we'll all die!"

Moving fast, Longarm put a hand on the tailgate and vaulted up into the wagon bed. He grabbed the man's shoulder and shoved him aside.

"Hold it!" roared Longarm. "Everybody stay right where you are, damn it!"

"It's that marshal!" someone called.

"We'd better listen to what he has to say," another man added.

Those voices of reason didn't stop the panic, but they

slowed it down a little. Longarm raised his hands for quiet, knowing he wasn't going to get much more, and shouted, "Those cavalrymen have orders to shoot anybody who tries to leave town! If you do, you're liable to get yourself killed!"

"But if we stay, we'll die anyway!" a man yelled up at him. "The doc said so!"

A chorus of "Yeah!" and "The doc said so!" washed over him.

Longarm waved his hands to get their attention. "That ain't what she meant! She's just as scared as the rest of you! But she ain't gonna run off, and you shouldn't either! You have to stay and wait it out! Only one man's died so far—"

"Tim's gonna die," said a man who had been in the saloon a few minutes earlier. "I saw him! He's got the sickness!"

"Yeah, but—"

The man in the wagon with Longarm shouted over his voice, "If we stay, we die! Simple as that! I'm gettin' out while the gettin's good!"

He jumped down from the vehicle and started pushing his way through the crowd. Most of the men turned to follow his example. The mass exodus had paused for a moment, but it was getting under way again.

"Damn it!" Longarm said. He leaped to the ground and grabbed the shoulder of a townsman who was trying to flee. "Hold on there, old son—"

The man jerked around. His face was twisted in fear-crazed lines.

"Let me go!" he screamed. "I won't let you make me stay here and die!"

The man threw a wild, roundhouse punch at Longarm's head. Longarm ducked under it and stepped in to launch an uppercut that slammed solidly into the man's jaw. The man went over backward out cold.

Before Longarm could raise his voice again and try to get the mob to listen to reason, something crashed into the back of his head from behind. The blow drove him forward. He stumbled a couple of steps before he caught his balance.

"Get him!" somebody yelled. "He wants to stop us!"

Men closed in around Longarm, flailing wild punches at him. He blocked or avoided as many as he could, but there were too many fists coming at him. Some of them got through and landed against his head and body with jarring impacts. He was rocked back and forth by the blows.

Longarm stayed on his feet as long as he could, knowing that if he went down, this loco bunch might kick and stomp him to death. His fists lashed out, knocking men away from him.

But for every man Longarm battered away from him, two or three more leaped to take his place. It was a losing battle. The odds against the big lawman were just too high.

Suddenly, someone jumped on his back. He staggered forward. A leg was thrust between his ankles. Despite his best efforts, Longarm tripped and felt himself falling forward. With the man's weight on his back, there was nothing he could do to prevent the fall.

Just as he figured would happen, booted feet hammered him brutally and ruthlessly. He hadn't drawn his gun before because he didn't want to set off a shooting spree that would doubtless leave a lot of people dead.

But now his life might well be at stake, so he made a grab for his Colt.

It wasn't there. The holster was empty. He knew the gun must have slipped out when he fell.

That meant all he could do was try to shrug off the

damage being done to him and fight his way back to his feet. He made a gallant attempt, grabbing a booted foot as it tried to kick him and hauling upward so that the foot's owner yelled and went over backward.

But again, the odds against him were too high. He was driven to the ground, and even though the street was dry, it felt like quicksand sucking him down. No, not quicksand . . . It was pitch that pulled on him, because it was black as night and twice as thick.

He sank into that blackness and knew nothing more as it enveloped him.

Waking up after he'd been knocked out was always something of a surprise. A painful surprise, to be sure, but a welcome one, because the alternative was death.

Longarm groaned and rolled onto his side. A hand clutched his shoulder.

"Don't move," a voice that he recognized as Amelia Judd's told him. "You could be badly injured."

Longarm ignored the warning and rolled on over onto his belly. He got his hands and knees under him and pushed himself up. Braced there for a second, he shook his head in an attempt to get the cobwebs out of his brain.

"Custis—" Amelia began again.

"How long was I out?" rasped Longarm. He opened his eyes and looked around. A few people still hurried here and there, but the street was a lot emptier than it had been the last time he'd seen it.

"Just a few minutes," Amelia said. "You might have been hurt worse, but that Farrar woman and Mayor McQuiddy showed up with the mayor's wagon. He drove it right through the mob to get to your side. That scattered them."

McQuiddy had saved his life, thought Longarm. The

men who'd attacked him weren't really bad hombres; they were just so scared that they hadn't known what they were doing.

That wouldn't have stopped them from killing him, though.

"Where's the wagon now?" he asked. He didn't see the vehicle.

"Over by the saloon. We're going to put Tim's body in it."

"Body?" Longarm repeated.

Amelia nodded. She looked like she was trying to hold back tears. "Yes, he . . . he died while you were out here trying to get those lunatics to listen to reason."

A couple of riders galloped past. Not far behind them came a buggy, then a buckboard piled high with belongings.

People were abandoning Panamint like rats pouring off a sinking ship.

Longarm pushed to his feet. He was unsteady at first. Amelia took hold of his arm to brace him.

"What are you going to do, Custis?"

"There's only one trail south from here. Everybody will take it, and they'll come up smack-dab against those horse soldiers. I gotta get out there and see if I can head off a massacre."

"You're in no shape to—"

"I don't have any choice." Longarm started toward the stable in a stumbling run. His steps grew stronger as his head settled down a little. He had a mighty hard skull, and it appeared that had come in handy yet again.

He heard Amelia take a few steps after him, but then she stopped and sighed in frustration. "I can't stop you, can I?" she called after him.

"Nope," Longarm replied without looking around.

He was still a little dizzy by the time he reached the

livery barn, but he was feeling better by the second. Maybe that was real, and maybe it was just a case of a lawman driving himself on because he knew how much responsibility rested on his shoulders. Either way, it didn't really matter, Longarm knew.

The only important thing was preventing the blood-bath that would take place if the cavalry opened fire on the panic-stricken townspeople as Captain Shaw had said they would. Longarm had no doubts that Captain Shaw would follow through with his threats if he didn't stop the panicked townspeople of Panamint.

Longarm was thankful his horse didn't give him any trouble as he put on the bridle and threw on his saddle, tightened the cinches, and rode out of the barn. He headed south out of the settlement along the trail that the fleeing settlers had used.

He hadn't gone far when he spotted the torches and lanterns burning up ahead, casting a wide circle of light over the semiarid landscape. In that flickering glare, he saw that the showdown he'd been worried about was taking place.

The citizens of Panamint, some on horseback, some in wagons and other vehicles, some on foot with quickly thrown together packs on their backs, had come to a stop facing a line of mounted cavalrymen. The soldiers held carbines, and they were obviously prepared to use their weapons when Captain Shaw gave the order to shoot.

Shaw was out in front of his men, sitting stiffly in his McClellan saddle and glaring at the mob. "Back to your homes," he was saying as Longarm rode up. "My orders are clear. I cannot allow you to leave Panamint."

"You can't stop all of us!" a man yelled. "There are too many of us!"

That was true, thought Longarm. The mob could trample right over those cavalrymen if they wanted to badly enough. Some of them would die in the process, sure as hell, but most of them would make it through and get away.

"My men will shoot—" Shaw began.

"So will we! We got guns, too, mister!"

"If you fire on the United States Army, you'll be considered traitors," Shaw warned grimly.

"And if we stay in Panamint, we'll be dead."

Longarm had intended to add his voice to the argument when he rode out here, but he saw now that he'd be wasting his time.

Nothing was going to stop people in the grip of such mortal terror.

One way or another, before this night was over, Panamint would be deserted, he thought.

And like a rock rolling downhill, that thought knocked another loose in his head, then another and another, so that it seemed like an avalanche rumbling through his brain. Everything that hadn't made sense to him before was suddenly crystal clear.

He knew why Gideon Horne and Tim had died. He knew where the sickness infecting Panamint had come from and why no one else had fallen prey to it. The answers had been right there in front of him all along. He had suspected something a time or two, but now he was sure.

"Damn it, what's it gonna be?" a man shouted as the crowd surged forward. "Are you gonna get out of our way, or do we shoot our way outta this pestilent hell-hole?"

Shaw's narrow face looked like it had been chipped out of granite. But after a moment, his shoulders sagged slightly.

"I can't order my men to fire on their fellow Americans," he said. "Sooner or later you people will have to answer to justice, but I won't stop you. Heaven help you, though, if you spread this disease all over the Southwest. It'll be on your heads." Shaw wheeled his horse and raised his voice as he began issuing orders. "Make way! Clear the trail!"

The troopers lowered their carbines and began moving aside. As soon as there was a big enough gap, several men on horseback galloped through it. Other riders followed, and as the gap widened, wagons, buggies, and buckboards rolled forward to continue the pilgrimage.

At the back of the mob, Longarm turned his horse and headed for town again. There was nothing he could do here.

The final act of this drama would have to play out in Panamint itself.

Chapter 16

Amelia must have heard Longarm's horse, because she hurried out into the road and lifted a hand to stop him as he approached.

He reined the animal to a stop. Amelia looked up at him and asked, "What happened? I didn't hear any gunfire. Are the townspeople coming back?"

Longarm shook his head. "Nope. Shaw backed down. He ordered his men to move aside and let them through."

Amelia's shoulders slumped. She shook her head and said in a dull voice, "Then it's over. Whatever happens will just have to happen." She raised her head to look at Longarm again. "You should go with them."

He frowned. "What?"

"Well, there's no point in you staying here now, is there?" She gave a hollow laugh. "All of those possibly infected people are already out there. What difference do one or two more make? We should both leave Panamint. There's no reason for us to stay."

She made a compelling argument, but it was one that Longarm couldn't accept. "I reckon there's still a few people here. I didn't see Mayor McQuiddy in that mob, or Dallas."

"The Farrar woman can take care of herself. As for the mayor, if he wants to be a stubborn fool, I don't suppose there's anything we can do about that. He'll be the mayor of a ghost town soon enough."

Longarm swung down from the saddle. "Well, I ain't goin'. I never let anything stampede me in my life, and I don't aim to start now."

Amelia looked like she wanted to argue, but at that moment, someone called, "Custis!"

Longarm turned his head and saw Dallas, Clancy, and McQuiddy hurrying toward them.

Amelia made a face. Her dislike of Dallas was obvious, and from the glare that Dallas briefly sent her way, the feeling was entirely mutual.

For the most part, Dallas's attention was focused on Longarm, though. She gripped his arm and asked worriedly, "Are you all right, Custis?"

"Head still aches a mite," he replied with a nod, "but I'll be just fine."

"What happened?" McQuiddy asked, then he echoed Amelia's other question by saying, "Did the army stop them? Are the people coming back?"

Longarm shook his head and told them about the showdown between the townspeople and the cavalry.

"I can't believe they'd just abandon everything," muttered McQuiddy.

"When folks are scared enough, they don't think about anything except gettin' someplace where they hope they'll be safe. That's what happened here. Everything that's happened over the past few days finally just drove people over the edge. Tim gettin' sick like that was the last straw."

"Speaking of Tim, we'll have to bury him in the morning, like we did Horne."

Longarm nodded. "Yeah, I reckon so." He turned to Dallas again. "What about the girls who work for you?"

"They left with everybody else," she said. "I couldn't have made them stay if I'd wanted to, and I didn't want to." Her hand tightened on his arm. "Custis, we should leave, too."

"That's what I told him," Amelia said coolly. "He's being stubborn, though."

"I just don't much cotton to the idea of runnin' away," said Longarm.

"Neither do I," McQuiddy said. "This is my town, dammit, and I'm going to stay right here until this crisis is over, one way or the other."

Amelia looked around the empty town of Panamint. "I'd say it already is."

"Well, then . . . I'll stay until the people come back. They're bound to, sooner or later, once they realize how utterly foolish they were."

"And if Custis is staying here, I'm not going anywhere either," Dallas declared with a somewhat rebellious glance in Amelia's direction.

Clancy said, "I'll not be goin' anywhere unless the lass is goin', too."

The doctor sighed and shook her head. "If we're all staying, we might as well go inside and be comfortable," she said. "I have a pot of coffee on."

"That sounds good," McQuiddy told her with a smile. "Thanks, Doctor."

Dallas said, "I think I'll go back to the Copper Queen."

"No, come with us," Amelia urged. When Dallas looked surprised at that, Amelia went on, "As long as we're the only ones left in town, I think we should stay together. I realize that you and I don't know each other very well, Miss Farrar, but we probably have more in common than you realize."

"What do you mean by that?" Dallas asked with a frown.

Longarm could think of one thing the ladies had in common, but he didn't want to bring it up right now.

"Well, we're both women in a profession dominated by men," Amelia said. "I'm a doctor, and you run a saloon. Given that, we really shouldn't be enemies, should we?"

Dallas shrugged. "I suppose not."

"Come on. Let's go try to relax."

The five of them turned toward Amelia's house. Longarm tied his horse at the hitch rail in front of the place.

"Where's your wagon, Mayor?" he asked McQuiddy.

"Parked in back of my store. Tim's body is already in the back, wrapped up in a blanket. The weather will be cool enough tonight that it should keep all right until morning."

Longarm turned to Amelia. "Any idea how come he died so soon after gettin' sick, when Horne hung on for a couple of days?"

"Well, how a disease affects someone depends largely on what sort of shape they were in to start with. Mr. Horne must have been stronger." Amelia shrugged. "Plus, a disease can change its characteristics somewhat as it travels from person to person. No two people are ever affected exactly the same."

"You must be sorry you didn't even get a chance to try to save Tim, what with him bein' your helper and all."

"Yes, of course. It's a great tragedy, but then this whole affair is."

Once they were inside, Amelia went on, "Make yourselves comfortable. I'll get the coffee from the kitchen."

Longarm ambled along the hallway after her as she headed toward the rear of the house. As they entered the kitchen, he smelled the aroma of the coffee coming from the pot on the stove.

Amelia opened a cabinet and took down a tray and four cups. Longarm said, "You're not havin' any?"

She looked back over her shoulder at him and smiled. "I've had so much coffee the past few days, I feel like if I drink another cup, I'll turn into a coffee bean."

She started to pick up the pot, but Longarm was there first, reaching his hand past her to grasp the pot's handle and lift it from the stove.

"Lemme pour that for you— Yow!"

He yelped in pain and let go of the pot. It crashed to the kitchen floor at their feet. The lid came off, and the black brew inside sprayed and splashed across the floorboards, forcing them both to jump back to avoid the hot liquid.

"Dadgum it!" said Longarm. "Look what I did. That blasted handle was hotter than I expected it to be. I'm mighty sorry about the mess, Amelia. I'll clean it up—"

"No, never mind," she said. "Don't worry, Custis, it's fine. I'm a doctor. I'm used to all sorts of stains." She picked up the empty pot and set it back on the stove. "I'll just make some more for the four of you."

A rumble sounded in the street outside. Longarm recognized it as hoofbeats from a large group of horses.

"Sounds like it might take more than one pot," he told Amelia. "You've got company."

She looked at the puddle of coffee on the floorboards and shrugged. "Maybe some of the townspeople have come back," she suggested.

Longarm knew that wasn't true. He said, "Let's go see what's goin' on."

They returned to the front room and saw Dallas, McQuiddy, and Clancy at the window, holding the curtains aside so they could peer out.

"It's the damnedest thing," McQuiddy commented as he glanced over his shoulder at Longarm. "Those cavalrymen have just ridden into town."

"Why would they come into town when they were trying to quarantine it?" asked Dallas.

Longarm could have answered that question, but before he got a chance to, Amelia stepped back suddenly and her hand went into a pocket of her dress.

When it came out, she had a small pistol clutched in her fist. She started to bring it up toward Longarm.

But he had been waiting for her to make just such a move, so he was ready for her.

His left arm swept around and struck her wrist, knocking her gun hand to the side. He brought his right hand up in a loosely balled fist that clipped Amelia on the jaw and jerked her head back. Her knees unhinged and she started to collapse.

Longarm wrenched the gun out of her hand and bent forward to grab her as she fell across his shoulder. He lifted her senseless form with ease and swung toward the others, who were staring at him in total, uncomprehending amazement and confusion.

"Out the back, fast," he snapped, "before they think to surround the house!"

They just continued staring at him until he barked, "Move or die!"

That got them to rattle their hocks, even though they were still clearly baffled about what was going on. Dallas led the way down the hall toward the rear of the house with Clancy behind her, followed by Mayor McQuiddy and Longarm bringing up the rear with the unconscious Amelia over his shoulder.

As they hurried out the back door, Longarm called softly to Dallas, "Head for the Copper Queen. We'll fort up there."

She nodded her understanding and set off along the alley behind the buildings.

Unfortunately, the saloon was on the opposite side of the street from Amelia's house. They would have to cross the street somewhere. Longarm hoped it would be far enough away that Shaw and the others wouldn't notice them.

Before they had gone very far, though, he heard yelling behind them and recognized Shaw's voice.

"They're gone! Fan out and find them!"

"Cut across now!" Longarm told Dallas.

She ran between a couple of buildings and angled across Main Street toward the Copper Queen. The three men pounded after her. Down the street, a shout went up.

"There they are!"

Guns blasted out several shots. Longarm saw dust leap into the air as bullets plowed into the street. A slug whined over his head.

Then the carbines fell silent as Shaw bellowed, "Hold your fire! Hold your fire, damn it! You might hit Amelia!"

Dallas bounded onto the boardwalk in front of the saloon and slapped the batwings aside. The others raced in after her. Longarm told the bartender, "Bar the doors, Clancy!"

The craggy-faced Irishman leaped to obey the order. He slammed the doors and dropped a heavy board across them into its brackets.

Longarm lowered Amelia to the top of the bar. She was starting to stir now as consciousness came back to her. He handed the pistol he had taken from her to Dallas and said, "Keep an eye on her. Any other doors except the back one?"

Dallas shook her head.

"No outside stairs?" asked Longarm.

"No."

"Good." He motioned for Clancy and McQuiddy to follow him. "Let's shove that piano in front of the back door. That'll keep those varmints out for a little while anyway."

The two men helped him without asking any questions. Once they had pushed the heavy piano into place, though, McQuiddy said, "I hope you'll tell us what in the blue blazes is going on around here, Marshal."

Longarm thumbed his hat to the back of his head and nodded. "It's liable to take Shaw a few minutes to figure out what to do next," he said. "He won't want to launch an all-out assault on this place, because he knows we've got Amelia in here. Reckon he'll try to keep her safe, at least for now."

"Why would he do that?" asked McQuiddy.

"Because she's his partner in this whole scheme."

Frustration and confusion were evident in the mayor's voice as he said, "This whole scheme to do *what*?"

"Why, to steal all those giant silver cannonballs down at the mill," said Longarm.

McQuiddy shook his head. "I don't understand. Shaw is a captain in the United States Army—"

"Not likely," Longarm cut in. "Maybe he was once. Maybe he's a deserter. Some of that bunch could be. Or maybe they're all just a gang of low-down owlhoots who stole those uniforms somewhere. They ain't the real cavalry, though, just like Gideon Horne and Tim didn't really die of cholera."

"They didn't? Then what did they die of?"

Longarm jerked a thumb toward the bar, where Amelia had come to her senses and lifted herself on an elbow to glare daggers at him.

"She murdered 'em," he said. "She gave 'em some sort of poison. I ain't a doctor, so I don't know exactly what it was, but she gave Horne enough to make him sick so he'd linger for a couple of days before dyin'. She fed Tim enough to kill him a lot quicker. I have my suspicion the same stuff was in that coffee she was gonna give us at her place, only I spilled it on the kitchen floor before she could. I was givin' her a chance to prove me wrong, but when she said she wasn't gonna drink any of it, I knew for sure I was right about what was goin' on."

"Well, I sure didn't have a clue what was going on," declared Dallas. She had stepped back a little so she could cover Amelia. The gun in her hand didn't waver as she pointed it at the other woman. "Is she a real doctor, or isn't she?"

"That I don't know," admitted Longarm. "She might be. She knows plenty about medicine, that's for sure. Enough to kill a couple of men and make it look like cholera, so the whole town would panic and go stampedin' outta here."

Amelia's face twisted with hate as she said, "You son of a bitch. You think you're so smart."

Longarm shook his head. "Nope. If I was really smart, I would've figured out what was goin' on a lot sooner. I had a hunch all along that something wasn't quite right, but it took me a while to remember what I read once about cholera, and an hombre named John Snow."

"Who?" asked McQuiddy. "I don't recall anybody by that name around here."

Longarm smiled. "You wouldn't, since he was a sawbones over in England. I make a habit of visitin' the Denver Public Library along toward the end of the month, when my wages have run out and I can't afford more expensive entertainment. I've learned some odd facts that way."

He didn't mention the good-looking young lady who worked at the library. He was right fond of her, and vice versa.

"Anyway, a while back, this fella John Snow figured out that cholera was spread by water, not just by bein' around somebody who was sick with it. You have to handle 'em, or the bedding they've soiled, or drink some water that the stuff's gotten into. You got a nice deep well here in Panamint, so I figured the odds of it bein' contaminated were pretty small. If Horne really had cholera, the one most at risk of bein' infected was the doc herself . . . and she seemed to be fine. So did you and I, after we handled the body."

McQuiddy looked at Amelia. "But . . . but she said we were all in danger."

"Sure she did. She came here a month ago to scout things out and make sure there was nobody in town who'd know better once she started spreadin' lies about everybody maybe bein' infected. Your old doc had died, and nobody else had any medical trainin'. She planned all along to poison somebody and make 'em look sick. Horne came along and gave her a perfect boogeyman. He had just ridden in, so she could even claim he'd brought the sickness with him and make it more believable."

"But what about that freighter who died at Fort Winston?"

Longarm shook his head. "There wasn't any freighter. That was just part of the story her and Shaw cooked up to scare you folks even more. The whole thing was calculated to drive the whole town into such a panic that everybody would just cut and run, leavin' everything behind."

"Like all that silver that was too heavy to steal easily," said Dallas, nodding as understanding dawned on her. "Good Lord, Custis! That means they've been work-ing on this for months."

"Yep," he agreed. "Lots of preparation, but for a mighty big payoff, too."

Dallas looked at Amelia. "I notice that you're not bothering to deny any of this, *Doctor*." Scorn dripped from the word.

"You could have avoided all this by leaving," Amelia snapped. "Now we'll have no choice but to kill all of you."

"You're forgettin' that you're in here and your part-ner's still out there," Longarm pointed out.

Amelia shook her head. "It won't matter, not in the long run. Jason will sacrifice me to get that silver. He'll burn the entire town to the ground if he has to."

"We'll just have to stop him."

Clancy spoke up. "How? There's a handful of us, and a couple dozen of those bloody outlaws!"

Longarm scraped a thumbnail along his jaw and ad-mitted, "I ain't quite figured out that part of it yet."

"What about that attempt on your life at the hotel?" asked McQuiddy.

"I suspect that was Shaw's work. He snuck into town last night to talk to Amelia and found out I was a lawman. He didn't want to take a chance on me bein' around to foul things up, so he tried to kill me. Maybe Amelia knew what he was gonna do, maybe she didn't. But when it didn't work, she told him to leave me to her. She'd take care of me."

Dallas snorted. "Not hardly."

Longarm refrained from saying anything about how Amelia had tried to distract him. Dallas didn't need to know about that.

"I knew I nicked the fella who busted into my room," Longarm went on, "and earlier today I noticed that

Shaw's got a limp. Now, one thing don't have to be con-
nected to the other, of course, but I'm bettin' that he's
hobblin' around because one of my bullets creased his
leg."

He looked at Amelia, thinking that she might confirm
his hunch, but she just stared back at him with hate-
filled eyes.

"But the cavalry—I mean, those men who are pre-
tending to be cavalry, you say—tried to keep everyone
from leaving," McQuiddy objected.

"Yeah, that was pretty tricky. Say you get somebody
so scared all they want to do is get out of a place, and
then you tell them they can't leave. That's just gonna
make 'em want to bolt even more. Shaw and his bunch
never really intended to stop anybody from leavin'. That
was just one more way to tighten the screws a little more
and make sure everybody panicked."

Dallas shook her head. "I've never heard of anything
more evil in my whole life. And you figured all this out
because you knew she wasn't telling the truth about the
so-called cholera?"

"That was the start of it," said Longarm. "Once I realized that, the rest of it just sort of started fallin' into
place."

Amelia sat up on the bar and let her feet dangle. "I
tell you, it's not going to do you any good. The best
thing you can do now is give up."

"And what'll that get us?" asked Longarm. "A bullet
in the head?"

Amelia's lip curled. "It's an easier way to die than the
way Horne and Tim went out."

Longarm couldn't dispute that.

He didn't make any reply, though, because at that
moment, Jason Shaw shouted from outside the saloon,
"Long! Marshal Long! Can you hear me?"

Chapter 17

All eyes turned toward the front of the Copper Queen, even Amelia's.

Longarm motioned for the others to stay back and warily approached the doors. He called, "Yeah, I hear you, Shaw! What do you want?"

"I want you and the people with you to come out! You're risking your life by remaining here where there's disease—"

"Forget it, Shaw! We know all about what you and the doc have been up to!"

Tense silence followed Longarm's words and stretched out for several seconds before Shaw replied, "All right, then. Do yourselves a favor and let Dr. Judd come out. I promise that if you do, we'll let you go. You can ride away, and no one will be harmed."

"So she's a real doctor, is she?"

"Of course! Now, will you come out peacefully?"

"I reckon we'll stay right here," Longarm called through the door. "Somehow I just don't believe you when you say you'll let us go, old son. Between you and the doc, you've already tried to kill me three times!"

Shaw didn't say anything to that accusation either.

Again silence filled the night while Shaw thought the situation over. When he spoke again, his voice was as hard as flint.

"Come on out, or we'll come in and get you."

Longarm began, "You're welcome to—"

Before he could add "try," a thunderous volley of gunfire smashed into the front of the saloon.

"Everybody down!" Longarm shouted as the glass in the front windows shattered under the onslaught and bullets began to buzz around the room like angry bees. He dropped into a crouch behind one of the tables and used his Colt to return the fire.

One revolver against a couple of dozen carbines wasn't much of a match, though, and he knew it.

He threw a glance toward the bar and saw that Dallas had tackled Amelia and knocked her to the floor. Dallas knelt atop the doctor now, pressing the pistol to the back of her head.

Clancy scrambled on hands and knees behind the bar and came up a second later holding a Winchester. He said, "Mayor!" and tossed the rifle across the room to McQuiddy, who had taken cover behind a table like Longarm.

McQuiddy caught the Winchester, swung the barrel toward the windows as he worked the lever, and fired. Like a lot of frontier entrepreneurs, he might be a businessman, but he had also fought Indians and outlaws in his time.

Clancy brought a shotgun from behind the bar as well and rolled over the hardwood with the Greener in one hand and half a dozen shells in the other. Longarm saw the burly bartender jerk and grimace.

Blood crimsoned the left sleeve of Clancy's shirt where he'd been creased. But he kept moving, advancing all the way to the left-hand window before he dropped to his knees, thrust the double barrels through the opening, and triggered off a devastating double load of buckshot.

The shooting outside stopped for a moment, and Longarm heard a man screaming. The cry died away into a bubbling sob. Somebody here in the saloon had successfully found a target.

"You got more ammunition behind the bar, Clancy?" he called to the bartender.

"Some. Not enough to fight off an army, though."

Longarm thumbed fresh rounds from his belt into the .44. Enough ammo or not, they might not have any choice except to fight off this particular army.

That, or die trying.

In the lull, Amelia said, "Let me talk to Jason. Maybe I can persuade him to let you go."

Longarm heard fear in her voice, and justifiably so. Her life was at risk, too, as long as she was in here with them. Clearly, she'd been right about Shaw being willing to trade her safety for the silver.

"You really think that'd do any good?" Longarm asked.

Amelia didn't answer.

Longarm grunted. "That's what I figured." He thought furiously. If the Copper Queen had been a stone blockhouse, they might have been able to defend it against the outlaws. As it was, sooner or later Shaw and his bunch would shoot the building to pieces or just set it on fire, as Amelia had threatened.

There was only one answer.

They had to get out of here.

By now, though, Shaw would have sent some of his men around back to cover the rear door. Trying to go out that way would mean walking into a barrage of hot lead.

Longarm turned his head to look at Dallas. "Is there a way to get to the roof?" he asked her.

"The roof?" she repeated. "Why do you want to get up there?"

"Because we can't stay here."

Dallas shook her head in despair. "There's no way, Custis. You might be able to climb out one of the second-floor windows and get up there, but I don't see what good it would do. We'd still be trapped."

Longarm's jaw tightened as an idea occurred to him. "Maybe. Maybe not." He turned to look at McQuiddy. "Mayor, you reckon you and Clancy can hold the fort down here? I hate to ask it of you, but if we're gonna all have a chance to get out of here . . ."

McQuiddy returned a curt nod. "Go ahead, Marshal. I don't know what you have in mind, but do what you have to do."

"All right. Dallas, we'd best tie and gag the doc there and stash her behind the bar where she'll be safe."

Dallas pressed the pistol barrel harder against Amelia's head. "Can't I just shoot her?"

"No, I reckon not. Sorry. I'd rather see her stand trial for murderin' Horne and poor Tim."

"Well, there is that to consider, I guess." Dallas jerked one of Amelia's hands behind her back. "Give me your other hand, you bitch, or I will just shoot you and be done with it. I have to tell you I'm hoping you'll give me trouble. I'd love to put a bullet or two in you."

Amelia put her other hand behind her back.

The firing from outside started again as Dallas hogtied Amelia with strips torn from her own petticoats. She pushed another wad of fabric into Amelia's mouth and tied it in place. Longarm hurried over to them, caught hold of Amelia's ankles, and dragged her behind the bar.

He wasn't any too gentle about it either.

Once that was done, he raised his voice over the roar of the gunshots and told Dallas, "Grab as many unbroken bottles of booze as you can find."

Bullets had already shattered many of the bottles, leaving the floor behind the bar awash in liquor. The sharp tang of alcohol filled the air.

Longarm found a box of shotgun shells and a box of .44-40s under the bar where Clancy told him to look. He tossed the ammunition to Clancy and McQuiddy, then turned back to Dallas and was surprised to see that she had taken off her dress and used it to form a makeshift bag. Bottles clinked against each other inside the dress.

"I've got a dozen bottles of whiskey, Custis," she said.

"That ought to do," he said with a grim smile and a nod. "Let's go." As they started toward the stairs, he called to McQuiddy and Clancy, "Give us some cover, boys!"

The two men picked up the pace of their firing. Longarm took the bottles from Dallas. They hurried up the stairs to the second floor.

Dallas led the big lawman to a bedroom on the side of the building. "Even if they're watching the back door," she said, "they shouldn't be able to see this window."

Leaving the lamp off, Longarm shoved the curtains aside and raised the window. Dim starlight filtered down into the narrow passage between buildings, but that was all. It was pretty dark outside the window.

"I'll go up," he told Dallas. "You'll have to toss those bottles up to me."

"I can climb up to the roof with you," she offered.

"That ain't necessary."

"I think it is. Strips from my petticoat will make good fuses. That's what you have in mind, isn't it?"

"That's the idea," Longarm admitted, grinning in the darkness even though Dallas couldn't see it. She had figured out right away what he was planning to do.

"Go ahead," she urged. "Just be careful, Custis."

Longarm took his hat off and dropped it on the floor. He could retrieve it later . . . if he was still alive.

Putting his head and shoulders out the window, he sat on the sill and tilted his head back to look up. From the corner of his eye, he saw reflected muzzle flashes from the street as Shaw's gang continued shooting at the salon. He heard both the sharp crack of the Winchester and the dull boom of the shotgun from inside, so he knew both McQuiddy and Clancy were still in the fight.

Longarm worked his way up until he was standing on the windowsill and holding on to the top of the window. He was glad he was as tall as he was, because the edge of the roof was just barely within reach.

He would have to grasp it and pull himself up by sheer strength, though. The only potential foothold was the narrow frame around the window, and it wouldn't offer much help.

Waiting wasn't going to make the chore any easier. He stretched his arm upward, clamped his fingers over the roof edge, and hung on as he reached to get a grip with his other hand.

The weight of his body was a tremendous burden for one hand to support. He managed to hang on until he got his other hand on the roof, which was a typical flat roof with a false front. Grunting with the effort of pulling himself up, he raised his body until he could catch a boot toe on the top of the window frame. That eased the strain on his hands a little.

Longarm dragged in a deep breath and heaved himself upward with both arms.

His head and shoulders cleared the roof. He drove

himself up and over and sprawled halfway on top of the building. His fingers dug in against the planks and pulled him the rest of the way.

The muscles in his arms and shoulders trembled slightly from the exertion. He would have liked to lie there and rest for a few minutes, but there wasn't time. Down below, McQuiddy and Clancy were probably running low on ammunition.

He rolled back to the edge and stuck his head and shoulders over. Reaching down as far as he could, he told Dallas, "Toss me the bottles."

She leaned out the window and took aim, then threw the bundle she had made out of her dress toward the roof. Longarm reached for it and snagged a flopping sleeve. Dallas had tied the sleeves together to secure the bottles inside the dress.

With a sigh of relief, Longarm lifted the bottles to the roof.

"Now me," Dallas said in an urgent half-whisper.

"You'll have to climb out and stand on the windowsill."

She did that, making frightened little noises as she balanced on the sill.

Longarm braced himself with his right hand and reached down with his left arm. "Grab hold of my wrist," he told Dallas as he wiggled his fingers.

"I . . . I can't," she said. "It's too far."

"No, it ain't. All you got to do is lift one hand and catch hold. I'll do the rest."

"Are you sure, Custis?"

"Trust me," said Longarm.

"Oh, Lord . . ." she breathed as she let go with her left hand and reached. Longarm clasped her wrist and she latched on to his and clung to it.

Then she lost her balance and swung out over the alley, supported only by his hold on her.

"Grab on with your other hand!" he told her between clenched teeth as her weight threatened to drag him off the roof. "Hang on, dang it!"

Dallas flailed her right arm for a second before she managed to grab Longarm's wrist with that hand, too. The muscles in his shoulders bunched and twisted under his shirt as he hauled upward. Dallas got a slipper-clad foot against the top of the window frame and pushed, which helped. He lifted her, reared up, then fell backward with Dallas landing on top of him.

She wore only a thin shift and her petticoat, so under other circumstances, Longarm might have enjoyed having her sprawled on top of him like that, but right now there was no time for such pleasures. She slid off him, rolled over, and stood up. Longarm was already on his feet, picking up the bundle of whiskey bottles.

"All right," he said as they hurried toward the front of the building. "Start tearin' strips off your petticoat."

She stopped and slid the garment down over her hips. "It'll be easier if I'm not wearing it."

That left her clad only in the shift. Longarm heard cloth ripping as she went to work on the fuses.

He used his teeth to pull the cork from one of the bottles. Taking a strip of cloth from her, he wadded it down into the neck of the bottle, leaving several inches dangling. He tilted the bottle so that the liquor would soak into the cloth.

Moving behind the false front, he looked out through one of the fake windows. The muzzle flashes winking like fireflies across the street from the Copper Queen told him where Shaw's men were located. A cluster of them were behind a parked wagon, so he selected that as his first target.

"Get some of the other bottles ready," he told Dallas as he fished a lucifer out of his pocket. Snapping the

match to life with a thumbnail, he held the flame to the
dangling end of the makeshift fuse.

The twisted fabric caught quickly and burned fiercely.
Longarm aimed and threw it at the wagon across the
street. Men yelled in alarm as they saw something that
burned flying through the air toward them, but they didn't
have time to scatter.

The bottle struck the side of the wagon and shattered
just as the whiskey inside it ignited. Flames splashed over
the men hiding behind the vehicle. They screamed as their
clothes caught fire.

The lucifer Longarm held was still burning as Dallas
handed him another of the crude bombs. Longarm set
the fuse ablaze and tossed it toward another group of
Shaw's men. It burst in their midst, spraying fire and
shards of glass.

"Up there!" yelled Shaw. "On top of the saloon!"

Longarm lit another lucifer and used it to set fire to
two of the fuses. He threw one bottle and Dallas threw
the other. They rained fire down on Shaw's men, who
had begun to break and run.

Longarm whipped out his Colt. Firing from the van-
tage point of the roof, he was able to drill several of the
fleeing men with steel-jacketed rounds from the .44.
They tumbled off their feet and didn't move again.

Renewed firing came from inside the saloon. With
Shaw and the rest of the gang scrambling to escape being pelted by the fire bombs, McQuiddy and Clancy had
had a chance to reload and regroup. Now the two men
cut loose from the windows, raking the outlaws with
buckshot and slugs from the Winchester. More of the
phony cavalrymen fell.

"We've got them on the run, Custis!" Dallas exulted.

"We sure do," agreed Longarm. Then he grabbed
Dallas's arm and hauled her down as he felt the wind-rip

of a bullet past his head. "Better stay low now," he advised her. "They're startin' to get in range."

He lit the fuse in another bottle and tossed it up and over the false front so that it fell and exploded in the street. If nothing else, it would distract the outlaws and also give McQuiddy and Clancy more light to shoot by.

The gunfire was beginning to die away now. Longarm heard hoofbeats and figured some of Shaw's men were lighting a shuck out of Panamint. They had realized that even a fortune in silver wasn't worth burning to death or being ventilated.

He stuck his head up and saw only a few muzzle flashes across the street. Most of the outlaws were either dead, wounded, or headed for the tall and uncut.

A scraping noise behind him made him whirl around. He saw a couple of shapes at the back edge of the roof. Two of Shaw's men had found a ladder somewhere. Only a careless step had prevented them from sneaking up on Longarm and Dallas.

"Stay down!" he told Dallas as he whipped up his Colt. The revolver roared and bucked in his hand as he fired at the shadowy shapes.

The phony cavalrymen returned the shots, Colt flame blooming in the darkness as they triggered leaden death at the big lawman. Then one of the men went backward off the roof as a slug punched into his chest. His arms windmilled as he screamed.

The thud as he landed in the alley behind the saloon cut short the yell.

The second man staggered and doubled over as a pair of Longarm's bullets ripped through his guts. His gun went off again as he fell, but the barrel was pointed at the roof now and the shot did no harm.

As the echoes rolled away, Longarm realized that all the guns had fallen silent.

He quickly reloaded, sliding the last of his fresh cartridges into the Colt's cylinder. A glance out the window in the false front showed him about a dozen men sprawled in the street. Most lay motionless, but some groaned and stirred. They were either wounded, burned, or both.

"Gettin' down's gonna be a lot easier than gettin' up was," he told Dallas. "Since those fellas were nice enough to lean a ladder against the buildin', we'll just use it."

Longarm kept his gun trained on the man who still lay on the rooftop as he and Dallas went past him. The outlaw didn't budge. A dark pool of blood surrounded the hombre, so Longarm figured it was safe to assume he wouldn't be getting up again.

Dallas went down the ladder first. Longarm followed. When they reached the ground, he led the way around the saloon to the street.

Putting out his left arm, he blocked Dallas's path. "I reckon the shootin's over," he said, "but we'd best eat that apple one bite at a time. You stay here."

"Be careful, Custis," she said, then chuckled. "It seems like I'm always telling you that."

"It's good to have somebody concerned about your welfare," said Longarm.

He stepped up onto the boardwalk in front of the Copper Queen. "Mayor!" he called through the broken windows. "Clancy! You fellas in there?"

Longarm heard feet crunching on splintered glass. "We're here, Marshal," answered McQuiddy. "Are you all right?"

"Yeah, I'm fine. How about the two of you?" Longarm knew that Clancy, at least, had been creased during the first volley.

"We both picked up a few nicks and bullet burns,"

McQuiddy replied, "but nothing to worry about. What about Miss Farrar?"

"She's all right, too. You still have ammunition?"

"Some. We were starting to run low, though, when fire rained down from heaven on those miscreants."

Longarm chuckled. "You sound more like a preacher than a politician, Mayor."

"Well, if tonight's not enough to make a man find God, I don't know what is!"

"Amen to that," muttered Longarm. "Come on out, but keep those guns handy, gents. We need to check on those varmints and make sure they ain't a threat anymore. We don't want anyone sneakin' up on us later."

McQuiddy and Clancy emerged from the saloon carrying the Winchester and the shotgun. Along with Longarm, they spread out and carefully crossed the street. Longarm checked on the bodies as he came to them. All the outlaws were either dead or unconscious now.

The ones behind the wagon and in the second bunch Longarm had targeted with a blazing whiskey bottle were all badly burned and dead.

Longarm's jaw tightened for a second. It was a bad way to go, even for an outlaw, but he wasn't going to lose any sleep over these no-good owlhoots.

"Marshal, are you *sure* about the things you said earlier?" asked McQuiddy. "I'd hate to think that we wiped out an actual cavalry patrol."

"They're phonies, all right," Longarm said with a nod. "Otherwise Shaw and the doc wouldn't have said the things that they did."

"That's true, I suppose. Speaking of the doctor, shouldn't we make sure she's all right?"

"Yeah, I reckon we should. Clancy, you go do that."

The bartender nodded. "Sure thing, Marshal." He loped back across the street.

Longarm and McQuiddy finished checking the bodies. They were still doing that when Clancy suddenly burst back out of the saloon and yelled, "Saints above, Marshal! Dr. Judd's gone!"

At that moment, a voice Longarm recognized as Dallas's let out a scream.

Chapter 18

He had left Dallas in the alley beside the saloon so that she'd be safer while he, McQuiddy, and Clancy checked on the outlaws.

Now it appeared that Longarm's caution might have backfired. He whirled and ran toward the alley, but before he could get there, Dallas appeared, stumbling out into the street with Amelia close behind her.

This time it was Amelia who had the gun pressed to Dallas's head, instead of the other way around as it had been in the saloon.

"Stop right there, Custis!" Amelia called. "If you come another step closer, I'll kill this whore!"

Longarm skidded to a halt. He raised his hands and patted the air in a placating gesture.

"Take it easy, Amelia," he told her. "You don't want to do that."

She glared over Dallas's shoulder at him and said, "Oh, you don't know how much I want to do that. That's exactly what I want to do. The bitch took such great pleasure in threatening me. Now she knows what it feels like to be on the other end."

"Killin' Dallas ain't gonna help you none, Amelia. You know that."

"No? What harm will it do now? I already murdered Horne and Tim. How many times can they hang me?"

Longarm shook his head. "They won't hang you."

"If they don't, they'll put me in prison for the rest of my life. That's even worse." Amelia shook her head. "No, Custis, I don't have a damned thing to lose . . . but I might have something to gain. I want a horse and a head start."

"You might as well ask for one of those giant silver cannonballs. You ain't gettin' that either."

"That's fine. I don't want one of them." Amelia smiled. "In his delirium before he died, Horne talked about where he hid the loot from that train robbery."

Longarm's jaw tightened. "And you think you're goin' after it," he said.

"I know I am, or this whore dies."

Slowly, Longarm shook his head. "I can't let you do it."

Amelia lost the tight control she was obviously keeping on her emotions. "Damn you! You'd better believe me when I say that I'll kill her."

Despite the obvious fear on Dallas's face, her lip curled in a sneer. "Don't believe her, Custis, not for a second. She's just trying to bluff you. And even if she's not, my life's not worth letting an evil bitch like her get away."

As Longarm watched the insane rage twist Amelia's face, he thought for a second that Dallas had pushed her too far. He believed that Amelia was about to pull the trigger.

If that happened, Longarm knew he would kill her a split-second later.

But that would be too late to save Dallas's life.

With a visible effort, Amelia controlled herself again. She said, "How about it, Custis? A horse for a whore. That's a fair trade, don't you think?"

McQuiddy and Clancy had come up behind Longarm. The mayor said quietly, "We can rush her if you like, Marshal. She can't get all of us."

"No, just stay back right now, Mayor," said Longarm. Suddenly too tired and angry to tolerate this standoff, he started walking forward. "We're gonna settle this right now."

Amelia retreated a step, dragging Dallas with her. "Stay back, Custis!" she said. "I'm warning you!"

"Put that gun down," Longarm snapped, out of patience now. "It's over."

"No! No!"

Then she did exactly what Longarm hoped she would do if he pressed her.

She jerked the gun away from Dallas's head and pointed it at him instead.

That gave Dallas the chance to twist around in Amelia's grip. Dallas's left hand closed around the wrist of Amelia's gun hand and forced it up, while her right elbow drove hard into Amelia's midsection. The gun barked as Amelia jerked the trigger, but the bullet went high in the air.

Longarm was about to rush forward toward the struggle when hoofbeats thundered somewhere close by.

He twisted toward the sound, palming out the Colt from the cross-draw rig as he did so. The horse loomed out of the night, almost on top of him. Longarm caught a glimpse of Jason Shaw in the saddle, swinging a gun toward him. Flame erupted from the weapon's barrel.

Longarm heard the bullet sizzle past his ear. At the same instant, his .44 blasted out two shots. The upward-angled bullets slammed into Shaw's chest and lifted him up and out of the saddle. Longarm leaped aside as the now-riderless horse pounded on past him.

Shaw had crashed to the ground and lay there struggling to reach the revolver he had dropped. His shaking hand was almost there when Longarm kicked the gun aside.

"Too late, old son," Longarm said as the phony captain lifted his head to look up at him. Blood welled from Shaw's mouth as his eyes went glassy. His head dropped, and he slumped onto his side.

Longarm knelt and checked for a pulse. He didn't find one. Shaw was dead.

As he and McQuiddy had looked over the bodies a few minutes earlier, Longarm had realized that they hadn't found Shaw yet. He hadn't known at the time that the leader of the gang had survived the battle. He wasn't surprised to discover that now, and since Shaw was dead, it no longer mattered.

The big lawman stood and turned toward the Copper Queen. Amelia stood there with McQuiddy and Clancy on either side of her. Each man gripped one of her arms. Dallas stood by, still dressed only in the shift, holding the gun Amelia had taken away from her earlier.

Amelia's head drooped in defeat.

"Is there somewhere in town we can lock that gal up where she won't get away again?" Longarm asked McQuiddy. "I'm gonna have to take her back to El Paso and see about findin' the money from that train robbery. Maybe Horne told her the truth, or maybe he was just out of his head and babblin'."

The mayor nodded. "I'm sure we can find a place."

"Let's see to it," said Longarm. "We don't need any more surprises tonight."

*   *   *

It was too late to go after the townspeople and tell them that it was safe to return to Panamint, that there was no cholera there and never had been. Longarm figured he would take care of that in the morning.

In the meantime, they locked Amelia in a sturdy smokehouse where she wouldn't be able to get out. She didn't bother cursing them anymore. All the fight had gone out of her after Shaw's death, and Longarm couldn't help wondering if the two of them had been lovers. It was clear that they had plotted the audacious ruse together.

When he was confident that Amelia couldn't go anywhere, Longarm returned to the Copper Queen. The saloon was dark except for one lamp turned low.

He went inside and found Dallas standing at the bar sipping from a cup. She wore a dressing gown now and had washed the smudges of battle off her face.

"You want some hot coffee, Custis?" she asked as she lifted her cup.

"That sounds mighty fine."

"With a little Maryland rye in it?"

He grinned. "Even better." He looked around the room as she went behind the bar to pour the coffee from a pot that sat on a small wood-burning stove. "Where are Clancy and the mayor?"

"Clancy's sitting up on the outside balcony with a shotgun. He says he's going to watch over the town tonight. Mr. McQuiddy's gone home, but he promised to come back and spell Clancy on guard duty later on." She handed Longarm the spiked coffee. "So you don't have to worry."

"I'm not worried," said Longarm. "More tired than anything else."

"Too tired to hold me for a little while?" Dallas asked

as she came closer to him, close enough that he could feel the heat radiating off her body. He could tell now that she wasn't wearing anything under the thin silk robe.

He smiled. "I reckon I can summon up enough energy to do that," he told her. "Just let me drink a little of this coffee first."

Not surprisingly, once she was in his arms and his hands began to play over her supple flesh, his fatigue went away. She tilted her head up to his and found his mouth with her lips. The hot sweetness of her kiss revitalized him even more.

"Maybe we should adjourn upstairs," he suggested when they broke the kiss.

"That's exactly what I was thinking," murmured Dallas.

Within minutes, they were in her bedroom and Longarm was peeling the dressing gown from her sensuous form. She tugged at his clothes with an urgency that made him shed them in a hurry.

When they were both nude, Dallas lay back on the bed and spread her thighs in eager invitation. "Ride me, Custis," she said with a throaty intensity that made his already-erect shaft harden even more. "After everything that's happened, I need to feel you inside me. I need to feel alive."

Longarm didn't want to even think about everything that had happened. He just wanted to concentrate on the here and now.

That meant positioning himself between Dallas's legs, bringing the head of his cock to the already wet entrance to her sex, and sheathing himself inside her with one powerful thrust.

Dallas moaned in pleasure as he filled her and lifted

her hips from the bed so that he was able to penetrate even deeper into her. Longarm launched into the universal rhythm of man and woman coupling, reveling in the sensations that rippled through him as his manhood slid slickly in and out of her.

His shaft throbbed as his arousal grew. Dallas bucked up harder against him, so he knew her excitement was peaking quickly, too. When she panted, *"More, more,"* he rode her hard.

Not surprisingly, neither of them lasted long as the tides of passion washed over them. Longarm felt himself being swept into his climax and didn't fight it because Dallas was already shuddering and spasming underneath him. His cock erupted inside her, his juices spilling out in spurt after white-hot spurt.

Dallas cried out and wrapped her arms tightly around his neck. Longarm kissed her, plunging his tongue into her mouth as they shared their culmination. The wave gradually passed, leaving them both limp and satisfied.

Longarm rolled onto his side and Dallas snuggled into his arms. Neither of them said anything. Now that their lovemaking was over, exhaustion claimed them, and they were both sound asleep within a minute or two.

Longarm awoke to the sound of a fist pounding on the door and Clancy yelling, "Marshal! Marshal Long! Are you in there?"

Longarm swung his legs out of bed and stood up as he instinctively reached out and snagged the Colt from the holster and coiled shell belt he had left on a chair next to the bed.

Clancy's shouts didn't necessarily have to mean that something was wrong . . . but Longarm wasn't going to bet on it.

"What is it, Clancy?" he called through the door.

"The mayor sent me to fetch you. There are riders headed for town."

Longarm's hand tightened on the revolver's walnut grips. It was possible that the members of the gang who'd fled had regrouped and were on their way back to make another try for the silver.

"I'll be right there," he told Clancy.

When he turned around, Dallas was sitting up in the bed, the sheet clutched to her throat. "What is it, Custis?" she asked.

"I don't know," he replied with a shake of his head as he pouched the iron and reached for his clothes. "I'm gonna go find out."

Dallas tossed the sheet aside and got out of bed. "I'm coming with you," she declared.

"Might be more trouble," warned Longarm.

"I don't care. I don't want to be left alone, and I can use a gun if I have to."

Longarm didn't doubt that. He nodded and said, "All right, but you do what I say."

Pointedly, Dallas didn't make any reply to that as she shrugged into her dressing gown.

A minute later, both of them left the room. Dallas carried the pistol she had taken away from Amelia. Longarm had his Winchester, which he had fetched from the livery stable after the earlier fight.

Dallas led the way through a door that opened onto the balcony on the front of the saloon. McQuiddy and Clancy stood there. The mayor was still armed with the rifle he had used earlier, and Clancy clutched the shotgun.

The sound of several horses floated through the darkness to their ears. The riders were approaching the town along the main trail from the south. Longarm's keen eyes spotted them as they reached the end of Main Street and started along it.

He counted six men. They rode slowly, warily, as if they expected trouble.

Longarm saw an unlit lantern sitting on the railing around the edge of the balcony. He motioned for his companions to be quiet. Taking a lucifer from his pocket, he waited until the riders were just about even with the saloon, then snapped the match to life and held the flame to the lantern. As the wick caught, yellow light washed down over the startled newcomers, who reined to a halt in surprise.

Longarm brought the Winchester to his shoulder and ordered in a loud voice, "Hold it right where you are, boys!"

Beside him, Dallas, McQuiddy, and Clancy leveled their weapons at the riders, too.

The first thing Longarm saw was that the men weren't wearing cavalry uniforms, stolen or otherwise.

With a shock of recognition, he realized that he had seen them before, though. The last time had been a couple of weeks earlier in El Paso, when he and Bert Collins were trading shots with them.

He was looking at the remnants of Gideon Horne's gang.

A grim smile touched his mouth as he said, "You fellas are about the last hombres I expected to see here in Panamint."

"You!" one of the outlaws exclaimed bitterly. "You're the fuckin' lawman who busted up our party at Mama Lupe's!"

"Watch your language, mister," Longarm warned. "There's a lady present." He gave them a steely-eyed look over the barrel of the Winchester. "What are you doin' here?"

"Looking for Gideon," replied the spokesman for the owlhoots. "What the hell do you think? He ran out on us and never told us where that loot from the train robbery was stashed."

Longarm chuckled, although he wasn't really amused. "Well, you're too late, old son. Gideon Horne's dead and buried, and the secret of where he hid that money was buried with him."

He didn't mention Amelia's claim that she knew Horne's secret.

"Yeah, we know. We ran into some pilgrims back down the trail who told us Gid was dead. Said the cholera killed him, and they were all on the run from the sickness." A wolfish grin stretched the man's thin lips. "We figured since they ran off and left their town empty, we'd come and help ourselves to whatever we could find. It won't be the same as getting our hands on that loot, but it's better than nothing."

"You'd risk getting cholera for that?"

"Hell, we've risked our lives plenty of times before for a payoff. This isn't any different."

Longarm knew that was true. These were buzzards in human form, existing only to live off the misfortunes of others.

"Yeah, it is different," he said. "This time you've run out of luck. You hombres are under arrest. Take your guns out, slow and easy, and throw 'em on the ground."

All six of the outlaws smiled, and the spokesman said, "You're outnumbered, lawman, and all you've got on your side are a couple of townies and a woman. A mighty pretty woman, at that. Try not to kill her, boys, and we'll have some fun with her after we're finished with these bastards."

"You ain't gonna surrender peaceable-like?" asked Longarm.

"What the hell do you think?" the spokesman snapped.

Longarm shot him in the head.

The round from the Winchester drilled into the center of the outlaw's forehead, jerked his head back, and exploded out the back of his skull in a spray of blood, bone, and brain matter.

The other survivors from Horne's gang clawed for their guns. Clancy's Greener roared, sweeping two of the men out of their saddles. Dallas and McQuiddy fired at the same time, but their shots missed as the outlaws' horses began to leap around, spooked by the sudden gunfire.

Longarm worked the rifle's lever and swung the barrel. He squeezed off another shot and saw a spurt of crimson in the lantern light as the .44-40 slug ripped into an owlhoot's throat.

Dallas and the mayor continued shooting, but the two outlaws who were still mounted had their guns out by now, and flame spurted from the weapons as they fired up at the balcony. Splinters flew from the railing as the bullets struck it. Dallas and McQuiddy were forced to retreat.

Longarm's rifle cracked again, and a third man fell to his deadly accurate aim. That left just one of the gang in the saddle. He whirled his horse as if to flee, but Clancy had reloaded by now and loosed another double load of flesh-shredding buckshot. Man and horse went down, both screaming in mortal agony.

In the echoing silence that fell as the gun thunder faded, Longarm lowered his smoking Winchester and spoke, directing his words at the first man he had killed.

"I think if you ain't gonna surrender, we might as well go ahead and start the ball rolling, you son of a bitch."

As the weary anger that had gripped him faded, he

turned to his companions. "Everybody all right?" he asked.

Dallas put an arm around his waist. "I'm fine," she told him. "Not a scratch."

"Same here," said McQuiddy. "No new scratches anyway."

"Aye, me, too," Clancy said. "What do you think, lad? Is anybody else gonna show up tonight and try to kill us?"

"I sure as hell hope not," Longarm said, and meant it with every fiber of his being

Watch for

LONGARM AND THE BETRAYED BRIDE

the 388th novel in the exciting LONGARM
series from Jove

Coming in March!

GIANT-SIZED ADVENTURE FROM
AVENGING ANGEL LONGARM.

BY TABOR EVANS

2006 Giant Edition:

**LONGARM AND THE
OUTLAW EMPRESS**

2007 Giant Edition:

**LONGARM AND
THE GOLDEN EAGLE
SHOOT-OUT**

2008 Giant Edition:

**LONGARM AND THE
VALLEY OF SKULLS**

2009 Giant Edition:

**LONGARM AND THE
LONE STAR TRACKDOWN**

2010 Giant Edition:

**LONGARM AND THE
RAILROAD WAR**

penguin.com/actionwesterns

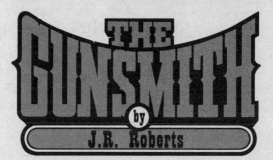

Don't miss the best Westerns from Berkley

LYLE BRANDT
PETER BRANDVOLD
JACK BALLAS
J. LEE BUTTS
JORY SHERMAN
DUSTY RICHARDS

M10G0610